The Mammy

**Center Point
Large Print**

**This Large Print Book carries the
Seal of Approval of N.A.V.H.**

ॐ श्री गणेशाय नमः

The Mammy

Brendan O'Carroll

Center Point Publishing
Thorndike, Maine

PUBLISHER'S NOTE

This is a work of fiction. Names, characters, places, and incidents either are the products of the author's imagination or are used fictitiously, and any resemblance to actual persons, living or dead, events, or locales is entirely coincidental.

This Center Point Large Print edition is published in the year 2000 by arrangement with Dutton Plume, a division of Penguin Putnam Inc.

Copyright © 1994 by Brendan O'Carroll.

The text of this Large Print edition is unabridged. In other aspects, this book may vary from the original edition. Printed in Thailand. Set in 16-point Plantin type by Bill Coskrey.

ISBN 1-58547-037-6

Library of Congress Cataloging-in-Publication Data

O'Carroll, Brendan.
   The mammy / Brendan O'Carroll.
      p. cm.
   ISBN 1-58547-037-6 (lib. bdg. : alk. paper)
   1. Fatherless families--Fiction. 2. Mother and child--Fiction. 3. Working class--Fiction.
   4. Ireland--Fiction. 5. Widows--Fiction. 6. Large type books. I. Title.

PR6065.C36 M36 2000
823'.914--dc21

00-024023

Introduction

The biggest influences on my life have been female. It just happened that way.

My mother Maureen retired from politics when I was just five years old. She was a socialist — the only TD at that time, to my knowledge, living in a Corporation house. From her retirement onwards, I had the undivided attention and love of a genius. She told me I could be anything I wanted to be, and I believed her and grew up with an unshattering confidence in myself. My father died when I was nine. She filled the gap admirably.

I have five sisters, Maureen, Pat, Martha, Fiona and Eilis. None of these went to school beyond fourteen years of age. Today, all of them are successful, and my pride in them is infinite, for they did this against the odds.

I was lucky to have been born in Finglas, Dublin, a place where strong women are in abundance. What I learned from neighbours and friends has taught me well what my mother meant when she said: 'The worth of a person is more important than what a person is worth.'

In 1977 I took one of these strong Finglas women for my wife — Doreen Dowdall became Doreen O'Carroll. To this day I am inspired by her strength of will, humbled by her kindness and often over-awed by her love for me and our three children. My partner and friend Gerry Browne also has a Finglas woman, Colette, as his wife. We never forget how lucky we are.

In the pages of this book, my first offering, is the tale of such a woman, Agnes Browne. I hope the reading of it gives you as much pleasure as the writing of it gave me.

I would like to take this opportunity to thank the following for their help, not just with this book but with my career in general: Gerry Browne, my partner in crime and passion; Pat Egan, a grumpy but lovable fucker, and a true friend; John McColgan, who only knows genius; Gay Byrne, for the leg-up and the push start!; Gerry Simpson, for getting on with it, and for the encouragement; Mary Cullen, for the proof-reading and the clobber; Tommy 'Eurovision' Swarbrigg, a real star; Buggsy O'Neill, there, even when there was nothing; Shay Fitzsimons, who's not happy until it's absolutely right; Gareth O'Callaghan, for taking the chance; John Sweeney, who gave me the first gig; Eamonn Gregg, a great footballer, and a great guy; Michael O'Carroll, my brother, for belief on top of belief — I love you; Tim O'Connor, a friend I never knew I had; John Courtney, a friend I always knew I had; Gabriel Byrne, who can encourage with a smile; Michael O'Brien who gave me a contract and an advance before he even knew if I owned a biro — your belief in me was inspiring, I hope I have come some way toward justifying it! My thanks to Ide, my editor (a tough job), and all in The O'Brien Press for your hard work. Well done! And to Evelyn Conway, my long-suffering secretary — thanks!

Finally, my thanks to Maureen O'Carroll, BA and TD, 1913-1984. She was me Mammy.

Brendan O'Carroll
Dublin 1994

The Mammy

'Brendan, just be yourself and the rest will come'
Doreen O'Carroll

This book is dedicated to
Gerry Browne
a man I care about,
and one who cares about me

Chapter 1

29 MARCH 1967 — DUBLIN

LIKE ALL GOVERNMENT BUILDINGS, the interior of the public waiting room in the Department of Social Welfare was drab and uninviting. The walls were painted in three colours: 'Government green,' as it was known to all in Dublin, on the bottom half, and either cream or very old white on the top half, with a one-inch strip of red dividing the two. The only seating consisted of two pew-like wooden benches — these were covered in gouged-out initials and dates. Lighting was provided by one large opaque bowl-like fixture hanging from a six-foot cable in the centre of the high ceiling. The outside of the bowl was dusty, the inside yellowed and speckled with fly shit. In the bottom of the bowl lay a collection of dead flies.

'Serves them right,' said the woman staring at the globe.

'What? Serves who right, Agnes?' her companion asked tenderly.

'Them, Marion.' She pointed to the globe. 'Them flies . . . serves them right.'

Marion looked up at the globe. For a couple of minutes they both stared at the light.

'Jaysus, Agnes, I'm not with yeh . . . serves them right for what?' Marion was puzzled and not a little concerned about Agnes's state of mind. Grief is a peculiar thing. Agnes pointed at the globe again.

'They flew into that bowl, right? Then they couldn't get out, so they shit themselves and died. Serves them right, doesn't it?'

Marion stared at the globe again, her mouth slightly open, her mind trying to work out what Agnes was on about. Agnes was now back scanning her surroundings; the wall-clock tick-tocked. Again, she looked at the only other person in the room. He was a one-legged man, half-standing, half-propped up at the hatch. She heard him making his claim for unemployment benefit. He was a 'gotchee', a night watchman on a building site. He had just been sacked be-

16

cause some kids had got on to the site and broken the windows. The girl was 'phoning his former employer to ensure he had been sacked and had not left of his own accord. Agnes was trying to imagine what it must be like to be sacked. Being self-employed, she had never been sacked.

'Fuck them.' Marion broke the silence.

'Who?' asked Agnes.

'Them flies,' Marion pointed. 'Fuck them, you're right, shittin' on everything else all their lives. Serves them right! Oh Agnes, is this fella goin' t'be much longer? I'm bustin' for a slash.' Marion had a pained expression on her face. Agnes looked over the man's shoulder. The girl was just putting the phone down.

'She's nearly finished. Look, there's a jacks outside in the hall, you go on. I'll be all right. Go on!'

Marion bolted from the waiting room. At the same time the girl returned to the hatch.

'Right then, Mr O'Reilly. Here's your signing-on card. You will sign on at hatch 44, upstairs in Gardiner Street at 9.30am on

Friday, okay?'

The man looked at the card and then back at the girl. 'Friday? But this is Monday. Yer man wouldn't pay me and I've no money.'

The girl became very business-like. 'That's between you and him, Mr O'Reilly. You'll have to sort that out yourself. Friday, 9.30, hatch 44.'

The man still did not leave. 'What will I do between now and Friday?'

The girl had had enough. 'I don't care what you do. You can't stand there until Friday, that's for sure. Now go on, off with you.'

'He's a bollix,' the man told the girl.

She reddened. 'That's enough of that, Mr O'Reilly.'

But he hadn't finished. 'If I had me other leg I'd fuckin' give it to him, I would!'

The girl bowed her head in a resigned fashion. 'If you had your other leg, Mr O'Reilly,' she snapped, 'you would have caught the children and you wouldn't be here now, would you?' She closed the doors of the hatch in the hope that Mr O'Reilly would vanish. He gathered himself together, slid the card into his inside pocket, put his glasses into a clip-lid box and propped his crutch under his arm. As he made for the exit he said aloud, 'And you're a bollix too!' He opened the door of the waiting room just as Marion got to it.

'That one's only a bollix,' he said to her and, surprisingly quickly, headed off down the hallway.

Marion looked after him for a moment and then turned to Agnes. 'What was that about?' she said as she took her seat beside her friend.

Agnes shrugged. 'Don't know. Did yeh go?'

'Yeh.'

'All right then?'

'I'm grand. Jaysus, the paper they use here cuts the arse off'a yeh.'

'That auld greaseproof stuff?'

'Yeh, it's like wipin' your arse with a crisp bag.'

'Yeh.'

'Well, what are you waitin' for?'

'I was waitin' on you to come back. Come

on.'

The two women went to the hatch. Agnes pressed the bell.

They heard no sound.

'Press it again,' said Marion.

Agnes did. Still no sound. Marion knocked on the hatch doors. Behind, they could hear the sound of movement.

'Someone's comin',' whispered Agnes. Then, as if she was preparing to sing she cleared her throat with a cough. The hatch opened. It was the same girl. She didn't look up. Instead she opened a notebook and, still with the head down, asked, 'Name and social welfare number?'

'I don't have one,' Agnes replied.

'You don't have a name?' The girl now looked up.

'Of course she has a name,' Marion now joined in. 'It's Agnes, after the Blessed Agnes, Agnes Browne.'

'I haven't got a social welfare number.'

'Everybody has a social welfare number, Missus!'

'Well, I haven't!'

'Your husband — is he working?'

'No, not any more.'

'So, he's signed on, then?'

'No.'

'Why not?'

'He's dead.'

The girl was now silent. She stared at Agnes, then at Marion.

'Dead?' Both women nodded. The girl was still not giving up on the numbers game. 'Do you have your widow's pension book with you?'

'I haven't got one, that's why I'm here.'

'Ah, so this is a *new* claim?' The girl felt better now that she had a grasp of what was happening. She lifted a form from below the counter. Both women shot glances at each other, a look of fear crossing their faces. They regarded the answering of questions on forms as an exam of some kind. Agnes wasn't prepared for this. The girl began the interrogation.

'Now, your full name?'

'Agnes Loretta Browne.'

'Is that Browne with an "E"?'

'Yeh, and Agnes with an "E" and Loretta with an "E".'

The girl stared at Agnes, not sure that this woman wasn't taking the piss out of her.

'Your maiden name?'

'Eh, Reddin.'

'Lovely. Now, your husband's name?'

'Nicholas Browne, and before you ask, I don't know his maiden name.'

'Nicholas Browne will be fine. Occupation?'

Agnes looked at Marion and back at the girl, then said softly, 'Dead.'

'No, when he was alive, what did he do when he was alive?'

'He was a kitchen porter.'

'And where did he work?'

Again, Agnes looked into Marion's blank face. 'In the kitchen?' she offered, hoping it was the right answer.

'Of course in the kitchen, but which kitchen? Was it a hotel?'

'It's still a hotel, isn't it, Marion?' Marion nodded.

'Which hotel?!!' The girl was exasperated now and the question came out through her teeth.

'The Gresham Hotel in O'Connell Street, love,' Agnes answered confidently. That was an easy one. The girl scribbled in the answer and moved down the form.

'Now, what was the cause of death?'

'A Hunter,' Agnes said.

'Was he *shot?*' the girl asked incredulously. 'Was your husband shot?'

'By who?' Agnes asked this question as if the girl had found out something about her husband's death that she didn't know herself.

'The hunter, was your husband shot by a hunter?'

Agnes was puzzled now. She thought it out for a moment and then a look of realisation spread over her face.

'No, love! A Hillman Hunter, he was knocked down by a Hillman Hunter — a car!'

The girl stared at the two women again, then dismissed the thought that this was Candid Camera. These are just two gobshites, she told herself. 'A motor accident . . . I see.' She scribbled again. The two women could see that she was now writing on the bottom line. They were pleased. But then she turned the form over to a new list of questions. The disappointment of the women was audible. The young girl felt it and in an effort to ease the tension of the two said, 'That must have been a shock.'

Agnes thought for a moment. 'Yeh, it must have been, sure he couldn't have been expecting it!'

The girl glanced around the room, wondering could it be possible that there *was* a hidden camera after all. Again she dismissed it.

'Right, then, let's move on. Now, how many children do you have?'

'Seven.'

'Seven? A good Catholic family!'

'Ah, they're all right. But yeh have to bate the older wans to Mass.'

'I'm sure. Eh, I'll need their names and ages.'

'Right! Let me see, Mark is the eldest, he's fourteen; then Francis, he's thirteen; then the twins, there's two of them, Simon and Dermot, twelve, both of them; then Rory and he's eleven; after him there's Cathy, she was a forceps, very difficult!'

'It was, I remember it well. You're a martyr, Agnes,' Marion commented.

'Ah sure, what can you do, Marion. She's ten; and last of all there's Trevor, the baby, he's three.'

The form had been designed to accommodate ten children so there was plenty of space left. The girl ran a line through the last three spaces and moved on to the next section. In the back of her mind she wondered what it was between 1957 and 1964 that gave Mrs Browne the 'break'!

'Now, when did your husband die?'

'At half-four.'

'Yes, but what day?'

'This mornin'.'

'This morning! But sure, he couldn't even have a death certificate yet!'

'Ah no, not at all — sure he didn't even go past primary!'

'No, a *death* certificate. I need a death certificate. A certificate from the doctor stating that your husband is in fact dead. He could be alive, for all I know.'

'No, love, he's definitely dead. Definitely. Isn't he, Marion?'

Marion agreed. 'Absolutely. I know him years, and I've never seen him look so bad. Dead, definitely dead!'

'Look Mrs . . . eh, Browne, I cannot process this until you get a death certificate from the hospital or doctor that pronounced your husband dead.'

Mrs Browne's eyes half-closed as she thought about this. 'So, if I can't get this until tomorrow, I'll lose a day's money?'

'You won't lose anything, Mrs Browne. It will be back-dated. You will get every penny that's due to you. I promise.'

Marion was relieved for her friend. She poked her in the side. 'Back-dated, that's grand, Agnes, so you needn't have rushed down at all.'

Agnes wasn't convinced. 'Are you sure?'

The girl smiled. 'I'm absolutely sure. Now look, take this form with you — it's all filled in already — and when you get the death certificate, hand them both in together. Oh, and bring your marriage certificate as well, you'll get that from the church that you married in. In the meantime, Mrs Browne, if you need some money to get by on just call down to the Dublin Health Authority Office in Jervis Street and see the relieving officer there.'

Agnes took all this in. 'The relieving officer, Jervis Street?'

The girl nodded. 'Jervis Street.'

Agnes folded the form. She was about to leave but she turned back to the girl. 'Don't mind that one-legged "gotchee". You're very good, love, and you're *not* a bollix!'

With that, the two women stepped back out into the March sunshine to prepare for a funeral.

Chapter 2

DUBLIN OF THE SIXTIES WAS — and in the nineties still is — a city of many sections and divisions. There was the retail section, the market sections, the residential section and the (now almost disappeared) tenements.

The retail section had two divisions — the southside and the northside — with Grafton

Street being the main shopping street of the southside, and Henry Street and Moore Street the flagships of the northside. A stroll through both sides of the city would leave one in no doubt as to which was the affluent side and which was not. The largest Cathedral is on the south, the largest dole office is on the north; the Houses of Parliament are on the south, the Corporation Sanitary and Housing sections are on the north. In a café on the northside, you can purchase a cup of tea, a sandwich and a biscuit for the price of a coffee on the southside. The River Liffey is the dividing line and even she knows which side is which as she gathers the litter and effluent on her northern bank.

Just ten minutes' walk eastwards from O'Connell Bridge along the quays and another three minutes' walk north, was St Jarlath's Street. The entire surrounding area for one square mile got its name, The Jarro, from this street.

Although housing some sixteen thousand people in the fifties and sixties, virtually everyone knew everyone in The Jarro. By

28

day, the area bustled with the movement of hawkers, prams and carts, as the men and women who lived in The Jarro made up ninety percent of the dealers from Moore Street and George's Hill. The Jarro also provided the labour force for both the fish and the vegetable markets, and the rest of the able-bodied men were either dockers, draymen, or on the dole.

Agnes Browne was one of the best-known and best-loved of the Moore Street dealers. She loved The Jarro. Happily, at 5am each morning, she set off with her pram, on top of which sat her folded trestle table, from her tenement in James Larkin Court. As she rounded the corner at the top of her cul de sac, her face would crack into a smile as she met the colour of Jarlath's Street, the washing hanging from a thousand windows on each side. She would pretend that this was bunting in all the colours of the rainbow, hung in her honour, for a variety of different reasons. She would invent a new one each day — one day she would be a film star, the next a war heroine, once she was even an astronaut, Ireland's first, returning to the cheers and adulation of her friends and neighbours.

Five intersections down St Jarlath's Street, where it joined with Ryder's Row, Agnes would meet up with her best friend and fellow dealer, Marion Monks. Marion was tiny, with a round face, golden hair and round 'clincher' glasses, that made her eyes look like two little black peas. To make matters worse, Marion had not one, not two, but three dark brown moles in a straight line just under her chin. Each had a healthy tuft of hair growing from it, giving poor Marion the appearance of having a goatee beard. It was at bingo one night when Marion's glasses broke at the bridge and she managed to finish the night only by holding one lens up to her left eye and writing with her right, that Marion earned her nickname Kaiser.

Together the two 'girls' would push their carts down St Jarlath's Street, sharing the cigarette Agnes had sneaked from Redser's packet. Agnes was married to Redser Browne for thirteen years, and never once had he offered her a fag. So, each morning for thirteen years, she had helped herself to one. Before reaching the end of the street, the two would cross the road so as to walk past St Jarlath's church, the church in which Agnes had married Redser and in which Kaiser had married Tommo Monks, a man twice her height and a legend on the docks as a hard man. Nobody would dare go against him, and yet he could be seen some nights staggering home drunk and weeping, as every couple of yards he would receive a slap of Marion's handbag, for inadvertently referring to Marion's mother as 'good old heifer-arse!'

When the women came to the front doors of the church, both prams would be stopped, and Marion would hand what was left of the fag to Agnes and climb the steps to the front door. She would gently push one door half-open and shout: 'Good morning, God . . . it's me, Marion!' Inside the church, five o'clock Mass would be in full swing. Of the thirty or so congregation, only the strangers would turn their heads,

31

the regulars were used to Marion's early-morning cry. The celebrating priest would not bat an eyelid, as he knew that, for her own reasons, Marion never attended Sunday Mass. This was Marion's way of praying, and that was that. The priest had seen it each morning for the eight years he had been in the parish and no doubt she would still be doing it when he was moved on. Marion would then descend the steps of the church and the two girls would round the corner and complete the ten-minute walk to the fruit markets where their twelve-hour working day would begin.

It is possible to buy almost anything in Moore Street with the collection of shops that are there, but on the stalls they concentrate mainly on fruit, flowers, vegetables and fish. Agnes and Marion sold vegetables and fruit. The two women would spend until half-past six at the wholesale fruit and vegetable market, getting their supplies. Of all the time they put in every morning in the wholesale market only a quarter of it would be spent picking fruit and vegetables, for by now the dealers knew well enough to give the two women the best of what they had — or pay the consequences. The rest of the time would be taken up in chatting, catching up on the local gossip and solving each other's problems, for here in the early hours of a Dublin morning one could find the remedy for rickets, the secret of how to make a greyhound run faster by rubbing its legs with a bit of turpentine in a rag, or the cure for a cut that had gone septic. Then, after a hot cup of tea and a piece of toast in Rosie O'Grady's Market Café, the two ladies would push their prams, still empty, down to the market, empty because they wouldn't take the fruit with them — Jacko, the box collector, would bring it down later on his horse and cart.

On arrival at Moore Street, the girls would go to the 'Corporation sheds'. These were gerry-built sheds, put up specifically for the use of the Moore Street dealers, to store overnight any fruit or veg that would go on sale next morning. The cost of a shed was five shillings a month. Agnes and

Marion shared a single shed and chipped in two-and-six each a month. Between seven o'clock and half-past, Moore Street would be a hive of activity, with stalls being set up all along the street. If the weather was inclement, canvas canopies would be erected to keep the dealers and the vegetables reasonably dry. Vegetables would be unbagged, fruit unboxed and apples polished, yesterday's flowers would be clipped again to give them fresh stems and the fishmongers would be scrubbing down their marble tops awaiting the arrival of the truck from Howth. By half-past seven Moore Street was like a country garden, beginning at the fashionable Henry Street end with a burst of posies from all over the world — roses, chrysanthemums, carnations and lilies, moving down towards the Parnell end with the various fruits and vegetables — anything from an avocado pear to a strawberry, in season, and finally, tucked away right at the end of the street, the fishmongers, where everyone could see them but no-one could smell them. This was the ritual each and every day, as dependable as a Swiss watch, as colourful as an American election, as noisy as an Italian wedding and as sure as a ride in the National Ballroom!

Not today! Agnes Browne would not be there today. Her stall in Moore Street would be bare, except for the wreaths laid around the bottom, placed there by long-time friends, Winnie the Mackerel, Bridie Barnes, Doreen Dowdall, Catherine Keena, Sandra Coleman, Liam the Sweeper, Jacko the Box Collector, Mrs Robinson and her twin stuttering daughters — affectionately called Splish and Splash. Today, Agnes Browne would be burying her husband. The grave was ready in Ballybough cemetery, the three pounds and ten shillings it cost thankfully being paid by the Hotel and Caterers' branch of the Irish Transport and General Workers' Union.

The children were all dressed up, the boys in grey corduroy pants provided by the Vincent de Paul, and white shirts and grey jumpers Agnes had bought in Guiney's, along with new underwear and seven pairs of plastic sandals. The money for this had been sent around by the hotel staff, along with a full breadboard of sandwiches and tiny little sausages. Cathy, the only girl, wore a black skirt and top, again sent down from Ozram House by the Vincent de Paul. Agnes was surprised to find she herself had a black dress at all . . . but it was drab and old-fashioned, so it was with great relief that she found that the one sent up, on loan from a neighbour, fitted her perfectly. She cut up her own dress into little black diamonds which she sewed on to the sleeves of each of the boys' jumpers. These black diamonds of death would be removed only after the first anniversary Mass for the children's father.

Since Redser's death, Agnes hadn't had a moment to herself. The previous night, the house seemed to be invaded by callers. Quietly and efficiently she entertained each caller, constantly making tea, offering a bottle of Guinness from the six cases sent down as a gift from Foley's Bar — Mr Foley had liked Redser, and Agnes. It seemed to go on and on. The younger children were taken down to

Marion's house to be bathed, and although Agnes had intended that Mark, Francis and the twins should have a bath at home, it was two o'clock in the morning before she knew it. The children had gone to bed, and she was exhausted. She tidied around the house, collecting the beer bottles and putting them back in their cases. She wondered if Mr Foley would like the empties back; if not she would send the boys down to the Black Lion with them and collect the three shillings per case on them herself.

Before going to her own bed, she checked on the kids. The younger ones, Cathy, Rory and Trevor, were in the single bed — Rory and Trevor at one end and Cathy's little face peeping out the other, flanked by two feet on each side. Their faces glowed from the scrubbing Marion had given them, and they smelled of carbolic soap. One of the overcoats that served as blankets had slipped to the floor and Agnes gently picked it up and placed it across the three children. The other bed, a double, had a huge eiderdown spread across it, one of Agnes's bargain finds at the

Saturday market on George's Hill — only seven and sixpence. It had been torn, and leaked feathers all the way home, but a few stitches and it was as good as second-hand! At the bottom end of the bed the twins slept side-by-side. She stared at them in wonderment as usual, for they always slept sucking each other's thumbs, spending their nights as Siamese twins. They had done this from birth and Agnes did not know if she could, or even if she should, try to stop them. They were not identical. Simon was taller that Dermot, and where Dermot had his father's mousey Browne hair, Simon was blond, with freckles in abundance. At the other end the large frame of Mark, the eldest, was sprawled across the bed. For fourteen he was big, big enough to be taken for sixteen. He looked rough and tough, a strong square chin, wiry muscular body and the beginnings of teenage pimples breaking out on his forehead — a forehead that Agnes could not see at this moment for Mark had his back to her, facing the wall. On the other hand, Francis's face was fully visible, the face of an angel. Pale-skinned and with fiery red hair, he lay on his back, his mouth half-open and a gentle hiss coming from his lips as he slept soundly. Agnes ran her fingers through the boy's hair and gently kissed him on the forehead. As she turned to leave, Mark's voice stopped her.

'Mammy.'

She turned, but he didn't.

'Yes, love?' she whispered.

'Don't worry, Ma, I'll be here.'

Her reply caught in her throat, and for a moment she closed her mouth and breathed deeply through her nose, then she whispered 'I know love, I know . . . goodnight.'

He did not reply and she left the room. This short exchange upset her, so instead of going to bed, she went downstairs and made tea. She had then slept fitfully in the armchair beside the dying embers.

Agnes regretted that now, as she stood in front of the mirror in her bedroom. There were bags under her eyes. People would think she had been crying! She hadn't, she didn't have time for it. She stood back from the mirror.

'Agnes Browne, look at you, a ragged auld wan!' she said aloud to her reflection. She was being hard on herself, for although she had given birth seven times in fourteen years, at thirty-four she looked thirty-four! Medium height with full lips and a button nose, she was pretty, her outstanding features being her raven black hair and chestnut-brown complexion around almond-shaped brown eyes, a legacy of her grandfather's visit to Spain . . . he returned minus a leg but plus a wife! A beautiful wife, for which most men in The Jarro would have given both legs for the chance to use the remaining one! She had died young, at only twenty four, of TB, but not before leaving behind three daughters, the loveliest of them being Maria, who became Agnes's mother. Agnes looked like her mother.

She heard a radio announcer say it was ten o'clock. She hurried down the stairs and gathered the children together. As she herded them out the door she noticed Mark was missing.

'Where's Mark?' she asked no one in particular.

It was Cathy who answered. 'He's in the toilet, he said he's not coming to Da's funeral.'

Agnes did not reply. She looked into Marion's face and in an effort to make a puzzled face, Marion turned the edges of her mouth downwards, gathering all the mole hairs together.

'Marion love, you go ahead with these,' suggested Agnes, 'I'll go up and see what's wrong with the little cur.'

She quietly climbed the stairs calling him, 'Mark, Mark Browne . . . get out here now!' By the time she had reached the toilet door there was still no reply. She banged on the door.

'Mark Browne, I haven't time for this messin'. You're going to Mass whether you like it or not. Get out of that fuckin' toilet *now!*'

The bolt clicked back and Mark emerged.

'What do you think you're up to?'

Mark did not look up. 'Nothin',' he mumbled.

'Then get down them fuckin' stairs and up to that church . . . and listen, don't you carry on today or I'm tellin' yeh, I'll swing for yeh! Do yeh hear me?' she was screaming.

Mark was already halfway down the stairs when he said 'Yeh'. They caught up with the rest of the family before they reached the church. Agnes straightened hair, pulled up pants and tucked in shirts, then the new widow and seven orphans entered the church as a pale and frightened family.

Chapter 3

IF THERE CAN BE SUCH A THING it was a great funeral. Agnes sat in the front pew during the Mass, flanked by Marion on one side and her seven orphans on the other. The children were pale from a mixture of fear, because they did not really understand what was going on, and excitement, because people kept coming to them and rubbing their hair and mumbling 'God bless you' or 'God love you, child', at the same time pressing money into their hands. The younger children would stare at the shining silver coins, wide-eyed. Not that they would have them for long, for after what he regarded as a respectable period, Mark gathered the coins from the children to give later to Mammy. The younger children would hand the money over without question, and Rory after some soul-searching, but Frankie would not hand his over under any circumstances. What Frankie had, Frankie kept — for Frankie! Mark hated his younger brother. Of all the children Frankie was the most selfish. He would never share anything he brought home with any of the others, yet if Mark got sweets from Mr McCabe, the local shopkeeper and the supplier of Mark's newspapers for his paper round, Frankie would sit there long-faced until Mammy insisted that Mark gave him some of them. Mark had often wished Frankie wasn't his brother. Frankie was Mammy's favourite. Mark understood that Mammies have to have favourites and he didn't mind that he wasn't it, but he couldn't understand that with children as cute as Trevor and Cathy, or even Dermo — cheeky but lovable —

Mammy had picked the only selfish bastard in the family to be her favourite, her pet. Mammies are blind, he supposed.

It was the meningitis that had started it. Mark recalled vividly the panic in the flat that night. The ambulance at the door, Frankie vomiting vile-smelling brown stuff. He could still see Frankie, eyes closed and beads of sweat all over his face, as the two ambulance men carried him down the steps of the building to the waiting ambulance. His mother was distraught, his father pale and shaking, not knowing what to do. They were taking Frankie to the fever hospital. Well, thought Mark, that's that. Mark had seen two of his uncles go into the fever hospital with TB, and they never came out again. The fever hospital, as every kid in The Jarro knew, was where you went to wait for God to collect you. He would never see Frankie again. As the ambulance pulled away, Mark remembered a kid coming up to him and asking, 'Who is it?' 'Me brother Frankie,' he had said. 'What's wrong with him?' the boy had asked. Unable to remember or pronounce meningitis, Mark simply said, 'He's fucked', and went back into the flat.

That night in his prayers Mark asked God to spare Frankie's life. God answered his prayer. Six weeks later Frankie was home — and Mammy waited on him hand and foot from then on! Even now, years later, when Mammy would ask Mark to go down the stairs to the coal hole for a bucket of coal, if Mark dared suggest that Frankie should take his turn, he would be met with a scowl from his mother and the usual reply: 'Remember the meningitis!' Mark learned a valuable lesson from all of this — don't be too hasty with your prayers!

As the priest announced that the Mass had ended a line of people formed, and one by one they shook hands with Mrs Browne and Mark, and patted the heads of the children. Almost without exception they would say to Mrs Browne: 'Sorry for your troubles', and to Mark: 'You're the man of the house now, good lad.' Mark understood this . . . well, nearly understood it. It meant, he thought, that he would be expected to take his father's place — bring in the money, protect the family, both of which he was prepared to do, and felt able to do. He worried, though. He hoped it didn't also mean that he had to sleep with his mother . . . he wasn't into that. No way!

The hearse pulled slowly away from the church. Behind it walked the funeral attendance, led by the Browne family. Mammy was flanked by her children, Cathy holding her left hand and Frankie linking her right arm. Mark walked behind her. He held Trevor's hand and beside him walked Rory, holding a twin in each hand. It was about a mile to Ballybough cemetery. On the way, the hearse turned down James Larkin Court. All the curtains on all the windows in every flat were drawn. The hearse stopped outside the Browne's front door. On the door a simple white card with a black border was pinned. It read: 'Redser Browne RIP.'

The hearse paused for a minute, then, with a growl, moved on again. They were within sight of the cemetery when Agnes first heard the hiss. She was puzzled initially, but then a huge puff of steam from the front of the Ford Zephyr — that was the hearse — announced that something was amiss with the vehicle. It stopped abruptly and the trailing crowd came to a ragged halt. The driver and his assistant jumped from the front of the vehicle. Some of the men went up to join them. There followed a communal staring into the engine, then a discussion about how far the cemetery was. The distance was a moot point. It seemed it was just too far to carry the coffin and yet the vehicle could not be driven for fear of damaging the engine. The decision was made to push the hearse to the gates and carry the coffin from there. More men were drafted from the cortege and, with a heave, the Zephyr lurched forward.

'Mark, what's in the box in the back of the car?' Cathy asked suddenly.

'Da,' answered Mark.

'Did he come back?' she asked.

'Come back? From where?' Mark looked puzzled.

'Mammy said Da was gone to heaven — he went after work. Did he come back?'

'Yeh,' Mark said.

'Why?' she pressed.

' 'Cause he didn't want to miss the funeral.'

Cathy's reply was a simple 'Oh', and on they walked, behind the now human-powered vehicle.

Kevin Carmichael had been employed for twenty-five years by Solemn Sites Ltd., the owners of Ballybough cemetery. He started as a grave digger, and over the years had worked his way up to cemetery manager. He loved his job and ordinarily the cemetery ran like clockwork. Of course from time to time little hiccups would occur: during the strike of '63 graves had to be dug by the family members, and once a well-known Dublin prostitute who was supposed to be laid to rest in the family grave, ended up, because of a clerical error, joining the Sisters of Divine Revelation! The mistake was quickly rectified and the prostitute's family thought it hilarious. Nobody ever told the sisters.

Today had all the makings of a bad day at the cemetery. Kevin prided himself on planning the arrival of funerals to be at least fifteen minutes apart, so as to give a semblance of privacy to each family. But a mixture of errors and circumstances saw three of today's burials arrive simultaneously. The Clarke funeral was running well behind schedule, due to the priest having had a heart attack mid-Mass. By the time an ambulance was called and a replacement priest found, Thomas Clarke (deceased) was indeed late for his own funeral, by one hour. The second funeral due in, the Browne family, was now arriving twenty minutes late — the reason for this was obvious as ten red-faced men pushed the huge Zephyr into the cemetery reception area. To top matters off, the O'Brien party were spot on time. So Kevin now had three funerals arriving together, and bedlam for lunch!

Fresh men were needed to carry Redser's coffin. Those who had pushed the hearse were knackered. Four barmen from Foley's pub were appointed pall bearers along with the two men from the funeral home. As the pall bearers moved through the now huge crowd, they joined the other two coffins, also being carried shoulder-high. With all three coffins in a row the procession began and everything went well for a while, the huge crowd following the three coffins — it looked like a mass funeral. Suddenly, one of the coffins broke ranks and took off down a side route. The crowd now rumbled with questions — 'Which one was that?' they all wanted to know. It was turning into a gigantic version of the Shell game. A decision was made by someone and a large portion of the crowd broke away in pursuit of the stray coffin. The children looked to Agnes for guidance, and, decisive as always, Agnes said: 'Follow the one on the left . . . that's your Da!' The words 'the one on the left' went through the crowd like Chinese whispers. At the next junction 'the one on the left' veered to the left again and up a small hill. Agnes and the children followed, so did the crowd.

After some five hundred yards or so the coffin was laid across two planks on top of the grave. The crowd milled around this spot and when everybody was in position, there was a deathly quiet. 'Our father who art in heaven . . .' the priest began, like the first singer at a singsong. The huge crowd joined in and Agnes wiped a tear from her eye. The children huddled close to her, and this made her feel a little less lonely. She glanced around at the crowd. Old friends were there and there were also a good few she didn't recognise, but Redser was a popular man. On the far side of the grave she picked out an attractive-looking woman who, like herself, was dressed in black, and was sobbing. Agnes didn't recognise her. At first she was puzzled, then slowly it began to creep in — the suspicion for the first time in her life that Redser Browne might have been having an affair. As the prayer ended, and the coffin was lowered into the grave, Agnes muttered under her breath: 'Yeh dirty bastard.'

Meanwhile, only four hundred yards away, the real Redser Browne was buried with just four men in attendance. Fittingly, they were all barmen from Foley's pub.

Chapter 4

AGNES BROWNE COULD TAKE A LOT OF ABUSE. She'd had a lot of practice. She was beaten regularly by her father, she was beaten in school and of course Redser beat her, but at least he only beat her when he felt he had a good reason!

She never told anyone about the beatings from Redser. She tried once — the very first time, it was. They had just moved into the flat in Larkin Court and she was as happy as a lark. They got a bed from Redser's granny in Ringsend (she'd had it in the attic) and they had ordered a new formica-topped table, four chairs and a settee from Cavendish's in Grafton Street — two pounds and fifty pence a week over three years with a week free every Christmas. The table and chairs arrived on a Friday and although Agnes was disappointed that the van man hadn't brought the settee as well, he promised he would bring it the next day, Saturday. Redser ate his dinner off the new table that night. He hardly noticed it and his only comment before he pushed his plate away and went to dress for his darts match, was: 'It doesn't make the dinner taste any better.'

Agnes always rose early on a Saturday. She didn't have to work because she had an arrangement with Marion — Agnes looked after both stalls on a Friday and Marion did both on a Saturday, but still she would be up at 7am. That Saturday she boiled a pot of water and filled the trough to make a warm, bubbly bath. She bathed Mark and dressed him. Then at exactly half-past eight, she carried Mark and his go-car down the stairs, strapped him in and headed for the second-hand market on George's Hill. The highlight of Agnes's week was her Saturday rummage through the mountains of clothes, shoes and bric-a-brac of this market. She knew all the dealers' nicknames and why they had them. For instance, 'Bungalow' was a retarded man that ran and fetched for the dealers. They sent him for chips or cigarettes or whatever. He got his name because, like a bungalow, he had nothing upstairs. On the other hand, Buddha, who sold bedsteads, buckets and sewing machines, was very smart and got his name from the way he spoke, every sentence beginning with 'But eh . . .'

This Saturday, Agnes just skimmed around the dealers instead of stopping, rooting and chatting, because she wanted to be back in time to meet the van man with her new, her brand new, settee. She arrived back to the flat at about eleven o'clock. As she entered the building old Mrs Ward, who lived in the ground-floor flat, met her on the landing.

'Your fella's gone out,' she announced. Mrs Ward fancied herself as the 'Keeper of the Castle' and the residents of the building used to say 'you couldn't fart but she knew about it and by the time she was finished telling someone else about it, it was a shite!' Agnes didn't even look at her as she struggled up the stairs with child and go-car. She just replied, 'I know.'

'Overtime, is it?'

'No.'

'Gone up to his mother's?'

Agnes didn't reply, half because she was nearly breathless and half because she didn't want to. Failure to reply never stopped Mrs Ward, for even as Agnes was opening her door two floors up, she could hear the old bat carry on below: 'Hard to get them away from their mothers, these young bucks.' Agnes closed the door to a muffled: 'Oh yes, they love their mothers . . . love them!'

She plonked the go-car down and took off her headscarf. As she was unwrapping the baby she glanced over at her new table and chairs . . . lovely! The table was in a mess from the remains of Redser's breakfast. A dirty mug, the sugar bowl, a bottle of milk and the teapot scattered around, the butter with the wrapping wide open like a grease-proof butterfly, and half a loaf of bread. Agnes decided she would put young Mark down for his nap before tackling the mess on the table. Once the child was asleep she would have the whole afternoon to herself. Redser never came back from the bookies on a Saturday before the last race was over.

The fresh air had done Mark the world of

good, and he went to sleep quickly, his rosy cheeks puffing contentedly. Agnes came back into the only other room of the flat and went over to her radiogram — a bargain she'd got from Buddha for three quid. She selected six records from her pile, all Cliff Richard of course, and loaded them on the spindle, set the speed to 45 and flicked the Play button. The arm lifted, and a record made a little 'plap' sound as it hit the deck. Agnes began to pin her hair up as Cliff went into 'English Summer Garden'. She loved Cliff, and so did Redser. In fact, Agnes had noticed the letters C.L.I.F.F. tattooed across Redser's knuckles before she'd even seen his face on the night they had met.

Her hair tied up, Agnes attacked the mess on her new table. When the table was cleared, butter in the scullery, loaf in the bread bin, Agnes took a damp cloth to the table. On her first wipe she noticed them — four long straight gouges. They were made by the bread knife as it cut through the loaf . . . they were made by Redser. Her heart dropped. She sat down and ran her fingers over the cuts slowly, as if somehow this might heal the wounds in her brand new formica-topped table. But it didn't. As Cliff belted out 'In The Country', Agnes wept quietly. Her table was no longer new.

When Redser came home Agnes was sitting on her new settee. Mark was by the fireplace, a cushion under his head, and one of his cot blankets over him. He was awake, but contented to lie there in the heat of the fire watching the flickering flames dance from coal to coal. Usually Agnes would have noticed that Redser was in a foul mood, but today she didn't care. He didn't say hello, or talk to the baby, but took off his coat, threw it over one of the new kitchen chairs and opened the oven. It was cold and empty.

'Where's me dinner?' He spoke into the oven.

'Yeh cut me table,' Agnes said quietly.

'What?' The oven door slammed.

'Yeh cut me table.' Agnes's voice now went up a notch. 'Look at it!'

'Fuck the table. Where's me dinner, woman?'

'It can't be fixed, yeh know. Yeh can't fix formica!'

'Are you goin' deaf . . . Where's me fuckin' dinner?'

'I didn't cook yer fuckin' dinner. Now will yeh look at me table?'

'You didn't cook the dinner? Yeh *didn't cook* me dinner?' Redser advanced towards Agnes and she saw the warning signs. His bottom lip went white and began to quiver, his forehead began to redden and his temples to pulsate. She stood. He stopped. There was a madness in his eyes, they seemed to jump about. She went to speak. The slap, when it came, seemed vaguely familiar. He used the back of his right hand, the one with C.L.I.F.F. across the knuckles. It met the right side of her face full on, her head spun to the left towards the fireplace and her now wide-eyed and frightened son. She remembered. It *was* familiar. It was identical to her father's slap. She wondered if her Da had taken Redser aside and shown him how it was done, or did young boys get taught it in school? She tasted the blood in her mouth. She didn't cry. A man's slap had long since ceased to be a reason for Agnes to cry. She just slowly brought her face back to his. He was half-smiling, just like Daddy.

'I don't want to hear another fuckin' word out of your mouth until there's a dinner on that fuckin' table.' He walked to the table quickly. He slapped his hand on it. 'Here! Right here . . . on this table . . . *my* fuckin' table. Right?'

She didn't speak. She went to the cooker and prepared a fry. He turned on the radio and fiddled with the knob until the racing and football results were coming through loud and clear.

That night Agnes went around to her mother. She had to tell someone. She recounted the story as her mother was ironing her father's shirts. Throughout the story her mother barely looked up. When Agnes had finished, she awaited some gem of advice or even sympathy from her Ma. Slowly her mother looked up, and in her Ma's eyes Agnes saw a surrendered spirit.

'Well, love, you've made your bed — now

lie in it!' said her Ma.

Agnes never told anyone again, but over time she learned how to avoid the beatings and she also established an unspoken but well-understood law with Redser. She did this with a look, the way only a woman can, and the look said: 'I can take it . . . but don't ever touch my children.' Redser never did.

Chapter 5

THE MAY SUNSHINE CUT LIKE A BLADE down Dublin's Moore Street, the fishwives cursed the swarming flies, and Agnes Browne sat by her stall and reflected on the three months that had passed since Redser's death. Her first Easter as a widow had come and gone. She now collected her weekly pension along with her fuel voucher for two free bags of turf. The children had settled a bit, although Mark seemed to be uneasy, fidgety — 'a bee up his arse' her mother would have called it, maybe it was the . . .

'Penny for your thoughts,' a voice cut across her reflection. It was Marion, carrying two mugs of bovril.

'What?'

'Your thoughts, a penny for them . . . you were miles away.'

'Yeh . . . Mark!'

'What about him?'

'He's not himself.'

'Is he sick? Has he a temperature?'

'Ah no, he's as healthy as a pup. No, it's somethin' else.'

'What?'

'I don't know, I'm tellin' yeh. If I knew I wouldn't be worried, would I? Look grab yer woman, she's lookin' at your bananas!'

'Here, hold me mug.' Marion hurried over to her stall where a 'lady' was indeed examining Marion's wares.

'Can I help you, love?'

'Just looking, thanks.'

'Oh they love that, they do.'

The woman looked at Marion who was barely visible on the other side of the stall.

'I beg your pardon?' she asked.

'Bananas, they love it when you look at them.'

The woman held the stare, not knowing how to answer Marion's statement. She blinked and went back to the bananas. She picked up a bunch of six, turned them this way and that, and then replaced them.

'They look a bit pale,' she remarked.

'Yeh,' answered Marion. 'Ah they're probably dizzy, they had a rough crossing from Jamaica.'

The woman stared again at Marion, then moved on awkwardly. Marion scurried back to Agnes and took her bovril back.

'You do scare them off!' said Agnes.

'Ah me arse! Either she wants bananas or she doesn't, I'm not going to play twenty bleedin' questions! She was pokin' them and squeezin' them — they're bananas not mickeys, they don't get any better if you squeeze them!'

The two women erupted in laughter.

'Ah Marion, you're a tonic!'

They both sipped their bovril and watched the passing shoppers. Marion turned to Agnes and was about to speak, but stopped, as if she was trying to find the words.

Agnes waited. 'What is it?' she blurted out finally.

'What do you mean?' Marion asked innocently.

'What were you goin' to say?'

'Nothin'.'

'Yeh were, Marion, now what was it?'

Marion prepared to speak and Agnes waited. 'Do you miss it?' Marion asked finally.

'What? Miss what?'

'Ah yeh know . . . "It"!'

'The quare thing?'

'Yeh, the quare thing!'

Agnes thought for a moment, and took a sip of bovril. 'Nah.'

'Are yeh serious, not even a little bit?'

'Nope, not even a teeny bit . . . What's t'bleedin' miss? The smell of chips and Guinness being breathed all over yeh . . . his chin like bleedin' sandpaper scrapin' off'a yer shoulder and neck . . . and then the wait and the worry . . . am I gone again?'

'But makin' love, Aggie?'

'Love, me arse! Makin' babies, makin'

more worries, makin' shitty nappies . . . makin' him happy!'

'And you, makin' you happy too. You can't say you never enjoyed it?'

'Marion, will you get a grip! Enjoy what?'

'You know . . . the organism!'

There was a moment's silence in deference to the magical, modern-day word. Agnes sipped her bovril, and Marion glanced around sheepishly as if she had just spoken a national secret!

'I never done one,' said Agnes defiantly. 'I don't think they exist.'

'They do, I swear, Aggie. I done two!'

'What! When?'

'One two weeks after your Redser's funeral, on a Friday . . . and one last August!'

'Are you sure they were organisms?'

'Positive!'

Aggie sipped her bovril again, and Marion just sat glowing with the memory of her last statement.

'What were they like?'

'Massive, brilliant!'

'Ah be pacific, ascribe it!'

Marion pulled the crate she was using as a seat closer to Agnes. Agnes reached into her apron pocket and pulled out a pack of Players Navy Cut, and they both lit up. Marion took a drag, removed a piece of tobacco from her tongue with a spit, and slowly exhaled. Agnes waited expectantly.

'Well, first I didn't know what was goin' on! He was really drunk so it was takin' him longer than usual. He was bouncin' away, up and down, up and down . . .'

'I know how that bit goes, get to the point,' Agnes interrupted impatiently.

'Oh right! Well, I was thinkin' to meself, if this fella doesn't evacuate soon, he'll fall asleep! Next thing, I had this feelin' . . . a wave came over me . . . like gettin' ten early marks at the bingo and you know somethin' good is comin'! A shiver ran through me body, me hips started jerkin' all on their own. I closed me eyes and it was like an explosion. I could see colours burstin' in me mind . . . like someone set off fireworks! Without me tellin' it to, me mouth let out a yelp. He stopped and said: "Sorry, I didn't mean to hurt yeh." I could hardly speak. "Keep goin'," I kinda whispered, but he just rolled over and said: "Ah, you're all right, I wasn't in the humour anyway." He was asleep in minutes. I just lay there, and I don't know why, but after a while I started to cry . . . I wasn't sad or nothin', I just cried . . . gas, isn't it? That was it! What do yeh think?'

Agnes sat open-mouthed. Marion took another drag and again glanced around to be sure nobody was within earshot. Agnes was deep in thought.

'Was that the first one or the second one?' she asked finally.

'Both . . . They were nearly the same, except on the second one I didn't cry!'

'Did yeh tell him about them?'

'No way, are yeh kiddin'? He'd say I had worms or somethin'. Anyway, tell him and it would be all over the docks in no time!'

'Yeh, you're right. How long did they last?'

'Just a couple of seconds . . . over in a flash!'

'Jaysus, I could have had one, Marion, and not noticed it if they're that quick.'

'Nah, Aggie, believe you me, if you had one you'd notice it, for sure! Here, I'm off!'

Marion took the two mugs and went back to her stall. Within seconds her familiar cry could be heard all down Moore Street: 'Ten pee a pound a'da hard tomatoes.' Agnes sat and pondered Marion's story and the enthusiasm with which she had told it. Just before standing up to add her sales cry to the Moore Street melody, Agnes's thoughts were: Well, fuck you, Redser Browne, leavin' me with seven orphans and not an organism to show for it.

Chapter 6

THE BROWNE CHILDREN WERE AS DIVERSE as it was possible to be. Although they had been loved almost equally by Agnes and ignored equally by Redser, they each developed an individual personality.

Mark, the eldest at fourteen years of age, was the apple of his mother's eye. Like a lot of Dublin first-born children, he spent his early years living with his granny. A big, strong lad, Mark was not afraid of hard work. He loved to fetch and carry, and would do anything that he thought would please his mother. Mark was never to have his mother to himself as he grew up, with babies arriving in the house year after year after year. This he considered normal, and from the time he was six years of age, Mark was changing nappies and cleaning up after his younger brothers and sister. With the younger ones constantly pestering him, Mark never really appreciated babies. That was until after the gap between 1957-1964, when Agnes, for the first time in Mark's life, was not pregnant. He enjoyed this time and marvelled at how beautiful his mother was without the bump she always seemed to have. Then, of course, in September 1964 along came Trevor, an unexpected interruption in Mark's life, whom Mark hated before he was born, but once home Mark doted upon. For the first time, Mark really felt like a big brother. Now with the death of Redser, Mark would have to fill the vacancy of 'Man of the House'. In many ways Mark was ready for it.

The Jarro had no such thing as a playground. There were no specific areas for children to go and entertain themselves, with the result that children made their own areas and their own entertainment. There was no park in The Jarro, so football was played on the streets. Two piles of coats would be put down for goals and the goal-keeper's area estimated by the players. Each player, of course, had his own idea of distance, so whether the 'keeper was inside or outside his area gave rise to the most animated of arguments, and even punch-ups. With England winning the World Cup the previous year and World Cup Willie instilling a fever in young Dublin boys, football occupied most of the boys' time. Matches would be played in every lane, back street or main road, at all times of the day. Mark loved soccer and now at fourteen he was Captain of the City Celtic Under Fifteens football team. He was 'football mad'. When he wasn't working at one of his part-time jobs, Mark trained for or played football. Up to now that was his whole life.

Dermot, on the other hand, preferred boxing. The local curate, Father Quinn, had set up The Jarro Boxing Club, or the 'Back Street Bashers' as they called themselves, and Dermot was one of its first members. Dermot was not a tall lad, but for his size he was strong and had a heart like a lion. He was one of Father Quinn's star boxers. Inside the ring or outside, Dermot was renowned as a great scrapper. Even boys some years senior to Dermot would be wary of taking on this little tiger.

Frankie preferred neither boxing nor soccer, but just liked hanging around with the local gurriers, the 'ne'er do wells'. Frankie was one of those kids who had the knack of getting everybody into trouble but never getting into trouble himself. He would lead from behind, always coming out of tricky situations with his hands spotlessly clean, while those around him paid the price. It was clear from an early age that Frankie Browne would end up either a millionaire or in prison.

In The Jarro, the girls played skipping or

chasing, and their agility at both was surprising. During daylight hours, chasing was for girls only, but in the evenings it was played by both girls and boys and became 'kiss-chasing'. The rules of kiss-chasing were simple: the boys would chase the girls and when a girl was caught she must kiss the boy that caught her. Girls who were champion runners during the day ran a little less fast at night, depending, of course, on who was doing the chasing. Mind you, there were some girls who could walk around at a snail's pace and never be caught!

Mark and Dermot were good chasers — both were handsome young boys and had no trouble catching any girl they chose to chase. Frankie never played. He preferred to spend his evenings playing poker with the other gamblers under the street lamp. He was a good poker player and rarely lost, which naturally made him unpopular. Rory liked kiss-chasing but found himself confused — he never knew whether to chase with the boys or run with the girls. Often, he simply gave up and went home to play with his dress dolls.

In every family there are children with minor afflictions, and, unfortunately for Dermot's twin brother Simon, he had them all. On top of a stammer he had a lazy eye, with the result that when playing kiss-chasing Simon would seem to be looking one way and running the other and when he did catch a girl, by the time he got out: 'Gi, gi, gi, gi, gimmie a kiss,' the girl he had caught had got bored and gone off. To solve his lazy eye problem the eye doctor in the clinic had given Simon a pair of glasses with a leather patch over one eyepiece, but instead of straightening out his eye Simon now turned his head sideways, which gave the impression that he was hard of hearing, which he wasn't. If he went to the local shop on errands for his mother, Simon would turn his head sideways to the assistant when asked what he wanted, and sta, sta, sta, stammer out his request. Simon spent his early childhood with shop assistants roaring at him and talking to him in sign language, thinking he was deaf.

Cathy was the only girl in the family and, unlike a lot of single girls in big families,

Cathy wasn't a tomboy. She was dainty, pleasant and terribly pretty, if a little unimaginative. For imagination she depended on her best friend — another Cathy, Cathy Dowdall. It was Cathy Dowdall who came up with ideas, like the one she had of collecting door-to-door for a wreath for the late Mrs Smith. The fact that Mrs Smith was alive and well didn't bother Cathy Dowdall. The two girls collected two pounds and ten shillings and had a rare ould time for a couple of weeks.

These were the children of Agnes and (the late) Redser Browne. Through size alone the family was tightly knit. They would fight like cats and dogs at home, and call each other names, but outside the house they stuck together like glue. The rule in the Browne family was: 'You hit one, you hit seven.' Since March twenty-ninth and Redser's demise, little had changed in the Browne house. If anything, the house was less tense, and for a short time the children enjoyed being the 'poor little orphans' of The Jarro. But that soon wore off and life went back to as near-normal as possible. Pity was short-lived in an area that faced tragedy from day to day.

Chapter 7

'MAMMY!' DERMOT CALLED AS HE BURST into the flat. 'Ma,' he called again, now moving swiftly into the kitchenette. Agnes sat at the kitchen table with Trevor on her lap. Trevor was slurping up bread and sugar with hot milk poured over it — a mixture locally called 'goodie' — which was his breakfast. Dermot stood before her, a look of anguish on his face, his legs tight together and one hand firmly on his bottom. He was squirming.

'What's wrong with you, love?' Agnes asked him.

'Me gick is comin'.'

'Well, what are yeh tellin' me for? Do I look like the gick collector? Go into the toilet and do your gick!'

'Mark is in there.'

'Well, tell him to come out . . . Mark!' she

yelled, 'get outta that toilet and let your brother do his gick!'

There was no reply.

'Mark!' she yelled again. Still no reply.

'He's in there ages, Ma, he won't come out,' cried Dermot.

Agnes got up. 'Here, Rory, feed Trevor.' She walked out to the landing where the toilet was, followed by Dermot, who at this stage was holding his bum so hard that only his thumb was visible. When she arrived at the toilet door she listened first before banging on it. 'Mark, are you in there?' For a moment it seemed that there would be no reply, then there was a very quiet 'Yeh'. 'Well come out, your brother's in agony here . . . and if he shits in those trousers, I'll make you wear them tomorrow.'

There was a click and the door opened a crack. It was enough for Dermot, he bolted through with his pants half-way down his legs. Even as Mark was closing the door behind him a groan of relief could be heard from Dermot. Mark, eyes down, walked past his mother and made straight for his bedroom, closing the door behind him. Agnes followed him as far as the door and when it closed against her she stood for a moment in thought.

'What's wrong with him?' she asked of no one in particular.

Simon just looked at her and shrugged. Rory was too busy getting the last of the 'goodie' into Trevor.

'Maybe he has worms,' Cathy offered.

'Don't be so disgustin' you,' Agnes said.

'People do get worms in their gick, Mammy, Cathy Dowdall told me, and they do be miles long.'

'Shut up that talk about worms, and you stay away from that Cathy Dowdall wan. She's a bad influence. Brownes don't get worms and that's that!'

All went quiet again. Agnes gently rapped on the door of the boy's room. 'Mark . . . Mark . . . Mark?'

'Janey, Ma, you sound like a dog with a hair lip,' Dermot announced as he re-entered the flat looking much relieved.

Agnes made a swipe at him, 'I'll hair lip

you in a minute. What did you say to your brother?'

'Me? I didn't say anything.'

'You must have said something,' Agnes insisted.

'I said, eh . . . "Come on, Mark, me gick is comin' "', that's all.'

'Then why is he depressed?'

'It's not me, it's his willy,' announced Dermot. The other children giggled.

'Who? Who's this Willie fella? Has Mark been fighting?'

With this the whole group erupted into laughter, and even Trevor joined in. Rory's face turned crimson and Simon had tears in his eyes.

Agnes was furious. 'Stop that!' she screamed. The laughter died suddenly but the children were bursting to let it loose. However, seeing their mother so angry, they all held it admirably.

Agnes scanned their faces. When she felt she had everybody's undivided attention, she went on with her train of thought. 'Now one of youse is going to tell me where I'll find this Willie.'

Cheeks were puffing, tongues were being bitten and tears were streaming down Simon's face, who, even though not making a sound, was shaking with held laughter. The children thought they were going to hang on until Agnes announced: 'When I find him, I'll choke him.'

The burst of laughter could be heard on every floor and in every flat of that building in James Larkin Court. Dermot ran out of the building howling. Rory went into hysterics, so much so that Trevor began to cry with fright. Cathy followed Dermot out the door and Simon buried his face in a cushion on the settee.

Agnes swept Trevor into one arm. With the other, she picked up the spoon that Rory had been using to feed the baby and 'boinked' Rory on the head. Simon, who had nearly stopped laughing, roared again. Agnes went to the cupboard and pulled out the baby's coat. After silencing his cries with the insertion of a soother, she put the coat on the child and turned to the other two.

'Now, youse can take him for a walk. Rory, get the go-car down the steps and you, Simon, take him.' She handed the child to Simon. She then went to her handbag and fished out her purse. She gave some money to Rory. 'Bring me back some Tide and a pound of broken biscuits. Now, go on, off with yeh!'

The two boys scurried out the door, and as they made their way down to the ground floor, Rory said something to Simon and the laughter started again.

Agnes slammed the door. 'Little bastards, havin' a funny half-hour at my expense,' she said aloud. The flat was now as quiet as a butcher's shop on a Friday. Agnes went to the radiogram and put on an LP, Cliff Richard of course. She went to the bedroom door again and was about to knock, but decided to leave it; Mark would come out in his own good time. Instead, she began to tidy up and dust the little flat, sailing across the room on the musical waves provided by Cliff's voice. She opened the cupboard to return the duster just as Cliff began a soft, slow song. With the cupboard door open, she stood for a moment and imagined what it must be like to be married to Cliff — those twinkling bright eyes, that smile all of the time, his coal-black hair falling across his tanned face as she ruffled his quiff. Without realising it, she was running her hand through the dark grey strands of her up-turned floor mop. When she noticed this, she giggled to herself and said to the mop, 'Oh, I'm sorry, Cliff,' and with a swift brush of her hand cleared the 'quiff' out of the mop's 'eyes'. She took the mop from the cupboard and began slowly to 'lurch' around the room. She closed her eyes. Suddenly, she was in the ballroom of the Savoy Hotel in London. Cliff had just collected yet another award, the one for being the most hand-some, talented and loving singer in the uni-verse. He had thanked the audience and stepped from the stage. He walked through the thronging crowd and stopped by the table where Agnes was sitting. Without speaking he placed the award on the table and extended his hand to Agnes. Coyly she stood, and as the flash bulbs popped and the lights swirled, Cliff began to sing softly into her ear. The crowd parted and, alone on the dance floor, Agnes and Cliff were the couple of the century, as they floated around the dance floor.

Had a stranger walked into the flat at that moment they would have seen an attractive, dark-haired, smiling woman moving in slow circles, hugging a damp shaggy mop. They could not be faulted for wondering if it might be a good idea to call the home for the demented. This is what Mark saw as he stood by the bedroom door. The music came to a halt and Agnes opened her eyes and noticed Mark. She was both startled and embarrassed at the same time. 'My God, you gave me a scare,' she muttered and quickly went to the cupboard, replaced the mop and closed the doors. Mark did not move.

Agnes sat down at the kitchen table. 'Sit down, Mark,' she said gently. He did so sullenly, sliding on to the chair. 'Are you all right, love? You seem to be upset . . . tell me what it is, and, sure, maybe I can help. Are you havin' a problem?'

'Yeh,' he answered with his head bowed.

'Well, tell your Mammy. Come on, love. What kind of problem?'

'A willy one.'

'And who's Willie?'

'My willy.'

'What do you mean *your* Willie? Is he your pal?'

Mark looked up at his mother. Maybe she really was going potty. 'Me willy! What I use to do me pee,' he said, now pointing down at his pants.

Agnes panicked. She jumped up from the table and put the gas on under the kettle. Tea sounded like a good idea. It had never entered her head that she might have to explain to her sons what other uses a willy had. With her back to Mark, she calmly said, 'I see.' She sat down again. 'And eh . . . what's the problem? Is it sore?'

'No,' Mark answered, without the elaboration that Agnes had hoped for.

'Is it itchy?' she asked, not knowing why she was asking such a stupid question, but probably in the hopes that Mark would take the initiative and begin to explain.

'No.' Again, no elaboration.

'Well, tell me. Tell your mammy, what . . . eh . . . what's wrong with your willy?'

'There's hair growin' on it.' Again Mark had lowered his head and actually looked as if he was talking to his willy.

'Is that all? That's all right, son.' Agnes was relieved. A simple answer should put him right here. 'That happens to all boys around your age. It's the start of becoming a man. All young boys get hair on their willy.' Agnes was smiling as she spoke and Mark was looking at her. His expression was one of relief. Agnes was pleased with herself, she was a 'modern woman' she thought. Her son had asked her a very personal question and she was able to answer it without a hitch. Then came the dreaded follow-up question: 'Why?'

Agnes thought. The modern woman here would say: It's called puberty . . . soon your penis will be erect, and you will have dreams at night which will cause your penis to discharge a creamy thick fluid. This is called semen and is what fertilises the egg in the woman's fallopian tubes and makes babies.

Agnes stared into the face of her eldest baby. His eyes awaited her answer. The modern woman went out the window. 'That's to keep your willy warm when you go swimming.' She jumped up to the steaming kettle and over her shoulder she said, 'Now, out with yeh!'

Chapter 8

IT WAS THE TOWN HALL, community centre, entertainment complex and political debating arena, all rolled into one. To the sixteen thousand or so population of The Jarro, Foley's Select Lounge and Bar was the centre of the universe. The Foleys themselves were a country family. PJ Foley had spent his childhood on his father's dairy farm in County Meath. He and his brother JJ grew up with the smell of manure and the carbolic soap they used to wash the animals' udders before the milking, implanted in their sinuses. Their father, old PJ, was known throughout the county as the 'horniest whore to ever draw breath'. Everybody was surprised when Dolly Flannigan married him, but nobody was surprised when she started to walk like John Wayne. The entire village were speculating as to how long it would be before Dolly was walking like John Wayne's horse.

But fate is a peculiar thing, and Dolly Foley, née Flanagan, had always had her fair share of luck. Shortly after Dolly gave birth to her second son JJ, old PJ was to find himself standing in the wrong place as one of his forty-strong dairy herd let fly with a back kick that would do Bruce Lee justice. In the operation that followed, old PJ lost both testicles and the use of his penis for anything other than relieving his bladder. Dolly described him, when stripped naked, as looking like 'a woman minding a piece of chewing gum for someone'. Old PJ took to the drink, and Dolly and the boys ran the dairy farm. It was obvious to all that the younger boy, JJ, was a natural farmer and although PJ pulled his weight, his heart wasn't in it. Five days after PJ's twenty-second birthday, his father was found frozen to death in the middle of the pasture. He was stripped naked from the waist down and neighbours reported hearing cries during the night of 'Is that a prick or what?' as he ran through the herd of kicking cows. Foul play was not suspected!

The farm passed to Dolly and her sons, and both PJ and JJ were happy with the arrangement that JJ should take over the farm and PJ would receive the sum of £10,000 as full and final settlement. So, with those immortal words 'Fuck that, I'm off!' PJ Foley boarded a bus to Dublin in 1958, in search of his fortune. He purchased the run-down premises on James Larkin Street in The Jarro for £4,500, spent another £1,500 on the furniture and new linoleum, and watched with pride as the painter put the finishing touches to the sign which read 'PJ Foley — Select Lounge & Bar'. Over the following twelve years neither the custom nor the decor changed much. PJ Foley, thanks to the steady trade provided by the locals, prospered. His brother JJ went on to pioneer the Artificial Insemination Programme of the sixties and had such a keen eye for quality donor bulls that he became renowned as 'the best bull-wanker in the country' — a title his castrated father would have been proud of.

As well as a successful business, PJ Foley also found the love of his life in The Jarro — Monica Fitzsimons, a fiery, red-haired, befreckled girl from Limerick city. They courted for three years and married in Limerick. Among the locals that travelled down for the wedding were Agnes Browne and Marion Monks. Agnes was fond of both PJ and Monica, though a little wary of PJ. She wasn't sure that he hadn't inherited some of his father's prowess, and was very careful not to encourage him.

Agnes would drop into Foley's bar maybe three or four times a week, and always on a Friday night, when she and Marion would down a couple after the Bingo. PJ would pull and serve the first round each Friday night and this one was always on the house. This particular Friday was no exception.

'Now, girls, a bottle of cider and a glass of Guinness with blackcurrant,' he announced as he placed the glasses on the table in the snug.

'God bless yeh, Mr Foley,' Marion answered.

'Well, any luck tonight? he asked.

'Not a bit of it,' Agnes cried. 'If it was rainin' soup, Mr Foley, I'd be the one out there with a fork!'

All three laughed.

'Still, I suppose youse only go for the crack, eh?'

'Me shite we do,' Agnes answered, and again they all burst into laughter. PJ wiped the table, from habit rather than to clean it, and left the two women to their chat.

The Friday night chats were important to the women. The subjects were many and varied, ranging from how Agnes's children were progressing in school to who was bonking whom in the area. Tonight they began with a discussion as to whether or not the priests down in St Anthony's Hall were fiddling the Bingo. After some probing statements, the women decided that they were just having a run of bad luck.

'So much for your morning ritual,' Agnes said.

'Whatcha mean?'

'You . . . every morning shoutin' in the church doors . . . "Good mornin', God, it's me, Marion",' Agnes moaned.

'Ah now, Agnes, that's nothing to do with Bingo.'

'Still, you'd think with you shoutin' to Him every mornin', He'd give you the odd full house!'

'Ah now, Agnes, God has much more important things to be doin' than worryin' about my Bingo numbers.'

'Ah I know, Marion, I'm only jokin' yeh!'

There was a lull in the conversation. Both women took a sup of drink and glanced around the bar. Marion produced two cigarettes and they lit up. Agnes spotted a couple of lads from the fish market and gave them a wave.

'Who are they?' Marion asked.

'Nipper and Herrin' from the fisher,'

Agnes replied.

'Seem nice enough,' Marion commented.

'Ah they are. Nice lads — a bit wild, but all right.'

'Do none of them ever ask you out?'

'Will yeh go away with yourself, Marion, do you want me to be charged with baby snatchin'?'

'I don't mean them . . . any of the fellas down there.'

'Some of them do . . . but Jaysus, Marion, I wouldn't be bothered, I wouldn't.'

'Well, you're mad. For God's sake, Agnes, you're only young. You could marry again — you should.'

'Marion, would you feck off. What hero would take on seven childer? And anyway, I'm not sure I'd want to. Lord rest him, but I swear I've had a better life since Redser died, I have!'

'Ah, yeh need a man.'

'I don't!'

'We all do.'

'Well *I* don't — organisms or no organisms, I don't.'

That statement brought another lull to the conversation. It was Agnes who broke the silence.

'Did you have any more?'

'I knew you were goin' to ask me that. I shouldn't have told yeh.'

'I'm only askin'. I don't want the sordid details of your love life. I was . . . interested, that's all.'

There followed another lull, a puff on a fag, a glance around, a sup of drink, and then Agnes looked into Marion's face.

'Well, did yeh?'

'No. I'm giving them up.'

'After two? Why?'

'I'm not feeling well since I had them . . . and I'm after gettin' a lump.'

'A lump? What kind of a lump? Where?'

Marion blushed slightly. She glanced around the room furtively, to check that nobody was paying any undue attention to their table. When she was sure, she opened her coat and placed her left finger on a spot between her right breast and her armpit.

'Just there.'

She closed her coat quickly, picked up her glass of stout, and as she supped it she glanced around the room again to be sure nobody was watching.

'On your diddy?' Agnes was aghast.

'Shhh, for fuck's sake, Agnes, do yeh want to take an advert in the bleedin' paper?'

'Sorry . . . on your diddy?' Agnes's voice had dropped to a hoarse whisper.

'Yep.'

'What did Dr Clegg say it was?'

'I didn't go yet.'

'Why not?'

'Because if this lump is caused by me havin' them organisms . . . I'd be scarlet, that's the why.'

'Don't be stupid, he's a doctor, he knows all about organisms. It wouldn't bother him.'

'Do you think so?'

'I'm sure of it. We'll get Fat Annie to mind the two stalls, and I'll go down with yeh.'

'Would yeh, Agnes? Ah, you're a pal! I'll tell yeh, it's sore. Some days I can hardly lift me arm.'

'It's probably a cyst — that's it!' Agnes

sounded sure.

'Yeh, probably.' Marion was relieved.

'Mr Foley? Same again, please, and two packets of nuts.'

Chapter 9

LIFE WAS TAKING AN UPSWING FOR MARK and his interest in girls was beginning to dominate his waking and sleeping hours. Rory's interest, however, was confusing for him. What he liked most about girls was their clothes, the feel of nylons and he longed to try out their make-up. In school the other boys called him 'sissy', but not to his face. All of the other boys knew that Rory, 'sissy' or not, was still a Browne, and you didn't take on the Brownes.

This protection was not afforded, not directly anyway, to Cathy, being the only Browne girl in the girls' school. She attended the Mother of Divine Providence Girls' School in Ryder's Row. It was a strict school run by nuns. For ten years of age, Cathy was a bright child. She was also well liked by her classmates. Cathy was very pretty. Her shoulder-length, raven-black hair always had a shine, as did her large brown eyes that were barely visible beneath the fringe that always needed to be brushed aside. Indeed it was this hairstyle that was to lead to the incident that would later be referred to as 'the case of the fringe and the nun'.

That day, Monday, had started badly for Cathy. She awoke to Mark's call that it was eight o'clock. The warm June sun exploded into the room when Mark pulled the curtains back.

'Get up, Cathy,' Mark yelled.

'I'm up, I'm up,' she replied sleepily, trying to bury herself beneath the blankets.

'You're not up — now, get up!' he said as he yanked the blankets off her, leaving her lying on the bare bed in her nightdress.

'Ah Marko,' cried Cathy.

'Ah nothin'! Now c'mon, Cathy, get up.'

Mark made sure everyone was up before he left the house for school. He had been up himself since five o'clock with his mother, as he was every morning. He would do his milk round with Larry Boyle from quarter-past five to half-six, then it was around to Mc-Cabe's shop. He'd pick up fifty papers and run on his paper round, arriving back to the flat at about half-seven or so, have a porridge breakfast and get the others up, before he left for school at quarter-past eight. Although the school was only ten minutes away, he had to leave early to drop Trevor to his Granny Reddin in Sean McDermott Street. Granny Reddin would mind the three-year-old until Mrs Browne picked him up that evening.

Cathy rummaged through the underwear drawer. No knickers! She rummaged through the boys' drawer, Mammy often threw knickers in there by mistake. Nope! No knickers. She wandered out to the bathroom. The clothes-horse was full and, right enough, there was a pair of knickers on it, but they were damp. She stood for a moment, scratching her head. It's a pair of pinnies today, she thought. Pinnies were a pair of her mother's knickers, the slack gathered to the front and tied together with a nappy-pin. This kept the knickers from falling down or drooping. It looked awful but it worked, and they kept her arse warm.

After a slice of toast, Cathy left for school, in her pinnies. She skipped through the early-morning inner-city traffic and at the corner of Cathedral Street met up with Ann Reddin, her cousin. The two then headed up to Moore Street and Agnes's stall. Cathy liked to call there every morning on her way to school. Agnes had her daughter's 'lunch' ready for her — a sandwich of strawberry jam and a piece of fruit. She gave her the once-over and then sent her on her way. Cathy would eat the fruit at her first break and the sandwich for her 'big' break, when she would be given the tiny free bottle of milk, provided by the State, to drink with it.

With the little bit of sunshine, the sisters had turned off the heating, and the classroom was a bit chilly as Cathy and her thirty-two classmates stood to recite the 'Hail Mary' in Irish. After the 'Amen', they all said the 'Sign of the Cross' aloud and sat down. The teacher, Sister Magdalen, began to clean the blackboard. The chalk dust rose, and for a few moments was caught in the streaks of sunlight that came through the four long, sixteen-paned windows. Sister Magdalen started to write on the board.

Cathy, as was her way, held her head in one hand and glanced dreamily around the class. The framed Proclamation of Irish Independence was surrounded by the photographs of the signatories. They died for us, Cathy thought. Then there was a huge crucifix, upon which hung a sad Jesus, with blood streaming from his speared side. He died for us as well, she thought, wondering if anybody lived for 'us'. There were four pictures along the windowless east wall. Nearest the light switch was John F. Kennedy. He died. She wondered if it was for 'us' or did he just die? Next to him was Pope John the twenty-third, who was, according to Sister Magdalen, a good man who meant well. The first of the living was next: Éamon de Valera, President of Ireland. Cathy often thought that being President of Ireland must be an awful job, because Mr de Valera always looked so unhappy. She was glad she was a girl and never had to worry about becoming president! The final picture was of Archbishop McQuaid, a man to be feared, a man who held the keys of heaven and the power of hell. A shudder ran through Cathy. In two weeks she would make her confirmation and come face-to-face with Archbishop McQuaid. She was dreading it. If he asked her a question from the Catechism and she didn't know the answer, he would put her out of the church, and she would be damned forever. She pushed the thought from her mind and looked to the blackboard. The word 'doctor' was written there in large capital letters. Sister Magdalen spoke.

'The doctor will be giving all of you a general examination today. However, we shall not let that interfere with our lessons, or our preparation of you all for the Holy Sacrament of Confirmation. You will leave the classroom in groups of five. You may strip in the cloakroom down to your knickers, and then wait quietly on the seats outside the Tea

Room until you are called. There is to be no
. . . listen carefully! . . . NO talking. When
you are finished with the doctor, dress and
return to class quickly and quietly, is that
clear?'

There was a chorus of 'Yes, Sister Magdalen.' Cathy, however, was not one of the
chorus. She had gone pale. Strip! she
thought in a panic, strip to the knickers? She
was lightheaded. The nappy-pin holding up
her mother's knickers felt like an anchor.
She began to blush. Her hands began to
shake. She stared at the crucifix: Please,
Jesus, help me, don't make me take off my
clothes . . . please, Jesus, do something.

Sister Magdalen was speaking again. 'You
five will go first, and we shall go anti-clock-
wise from then on.' She was pointing to the
row of desks nearest the door. Cathy
counted the seats in groups of five up to
where she was sitting. She would be in the
fourth group. She had to buy time — she
had to get a seat that would put her in the
last group. She would then have a chance to
sneak out during 'big' break, which lasted

thirty-five minutes. This would be enough time to get home, dump the pinnies and change into her own knickers, which would be dry by now. Even if they weren't, better a damp pair than to be called 'Droopy Drawers' for the rest of her school days, and beyond!

At the eleven o'clock break, she went into action. During the ten-minute break she had approached all thirteen girls who would be in the final three groups. She offered her fruit, her sandwich and milk, but to no avail. By quarter-past eleven she was back in class, in the same seat where she had begun the day. Sister Magdalen had instructed the girls to take out their Catechism, and the learning of answers to Archbishop McQuaid's questions began in earnest. At twenty-past eleven there was a gentle rap at the door. Sister Magdalen crossed the room, her crucifix dangling from her waist, and opened the door. There followed a murmuring through the half-opened door and the good sister re-entered the room and announced, 'All right, girls, the doctor is ready for you. The first group — off you go!'

The first five victims rose slowly. It was as if they were bound for execution. They huddled together and trooped out the door. The lessons continued.

'Who is God?' Sister Magdalen boomed.

'God is our father in Heaven, the creator and Lord of all things' they all sang back.

Cathy watched the clock. The time ticked by.

'What is the Blessed Trinity?' boomed Sister Magdalen, this time her long, pale finger pointing at Cathy. Cathy stood up.

'There are . . ."

'Stop.'

'. . . three . . .'

'I said stop! Cathy Browne!' Cathy stopped and peered at the teacher through her fringe. The nun walked slowly towards her. 'How many times do I have to repeat myself to you?' She glared at Cathy. Cathy didn't know how to answer this question. The nun's arms shot out from under her bib and she held them out as if she were ready to be nailed to the cross. 'Do I look like a parrot to you?'

Cathy was tempted to answer: No, Sister, a penguin, but she knew better.

'I asked you, Miss Browne, do I look like a parrot?'

'No,' Cathy mumbled.

'I beg your pardon?'

'No, Sister Magdalen.' Cathy spoke louder.

'Good. So you know that I do not intend to tell you each and every day to get that hair out of your eyes, do I?'

'No, Sister Magdalen.'

'Well, do it!' the sister screamed, and the whole class jumped!

Cathy put her hand to her forehead and with a flick of her head, the hair flew back to leave her beautiful, but now frightened, eyes bare.

The sister smiled. 'Good, now, what is the Blessed Trinity?'

'There are three divine persons in the one God: God the Father, God the Son and God the Holy Ghost.'

The door opened and the first five victims were back.

'Sit down, Miss Browne,' Sister Magdalen said as she walked away from Cathy. Cathy sat, and her fringe dropped down again. She looked at the clock: twenty to twelve.

Christ, she thought, twenty minutes — not long enough! At this rate Cathy would be stripped before the big break.

Don't panic, she told herself, maybe the next group will be longer. They weren't. They were back in class before twelve o'clock. At sixteen minutes past twelve the third group returned. It was time. Cathy's group rose. She was shaking as she walked out. The corridor was empty and the five went without a word to the cloakroom to strip. Cathy undid the leather straps on her sandals and slowly began to remove them. Her breath was coming in short gasps. As she pulled off her socks the tears began to well up in her eyes. Suddenly a woman came into the cloakroom. She was a pretty woman — not a magazine model, but pretty. To Cathy she was an angel, for she said: 'Sorry, girls, the doctor is going on his lunch break, so go back to your class and you will be the first after lunch.'

Cathy was the first to be dressed. She returned to the classroom, and, as one of the group explained to Sister Magdalen what had happened, Cathy stared at the giant but sad Jesus and whispered, 'Thank you.'

The school yard was filled with screeches and yelps as the two-hundred-plus girls enjoyed the big break. In the middle of the yard a skipping rope was turning and a group were singing 'Down in the valley where the green grass grows'. These were the third-class girls. The fourth- and fifth-class girls were bouncing balls up against the side of the bike shed singing, 'Plainy a packet of Rinso', while the sixth-class girls were giggling and talking about sixth-class boys and who kissed who. Cathy Browne was oblivious to all of this as she stood behind the bike shed and plotted her escape, her only comrade her cousin Ann.

'Why do you have to go home?' asked Ann.

'I just have to, that's all. Now will you bend over?'

Ann bent over beside the railings to be Cathy's 'step up' on to the top. Cathy stretched her leg up and gripped the railings, 'A one, and a two and a . . . ' Cathy stumbled because Ann straightened again. 'But if you're caught, you'll be killed,' Ann announced.

'Ann Reddin, if you don't bend over and stay bent, I'll give you such a kick in the hole that me shoe will come out your mouth!' Cathy was angry. Ann bent over.

But even as Cathy was standing on her back Ann was still talking. 'If you're caught you better leave me out of it!' she grunted as Cathy pushed off her back and clambered over the railing. Cathy's feet had barely touched the ground when she took off, running flat out for home. Within ten minutes she was standing on the landing outside the flat. She pushed open the letter box and tugged the piece of blue wool that hung across it. She pulled the wool out and bit by bit the door key made its way to the opening. She quickly slid the key into the lock and opened the door. She ran to the sink. The knickers were dry! She changed into them rapidly, discarded the pinnies and in less than two minutes she was bounding down the stairs to the street.

Cathy arrived back at the school panting and perspiring. The children were still in the yard. She had made it! Or had she? She had no way back in. How could she have been so stupid? She hid in the doorway of the butcher's shop next to the school's main gate — a locked gate. The only person that had a key to that was the principal — her teacher, Sister Magdalen! A car slowly passed her and stopped at the gate. The wine-coloured car was polished and gleamed in the after-noon sun. A man stepped from the car. It was the doctor. He fished in his pocket and took out a key. Cathy saw a ray of hope. She stooped low and scurried along the plinth of the railing until she got to the gate pillar. The doctor was fiddling with the lock. Cathy's mind screamed: Please don't look over here, doctor . . . please . . . please. The doctor did not look over, but as the lock clicked open he spoke, as if to the gate: 'Wait until I am back in the car and then walk along the side of it as I drive in. I'll drive slowly.'

Cathy was stunned. The doctor pushed open the two large gates and as he walked back to the driver's door he looked straight at Cathy, smiled, and winked! Just before he sat back in the car he said, 'Home to change your knickers, then?'

Cathy was gobsmacked — he was a mind-reader! He wasn't, of course — but he had been doing the school rounds for fifteen years. He knew the story. The car moved slowly. Cathy, crouched, held on to the door-handle and crept beside it. As the doctor was locking the gates, Cathy was al-ready half-way across the yard. She looked back at him and he was still smiling. She waved. He nodded. The bell rang.

Cathy put her tongue out as far as it would go. The doctor pressed the lollipop stick down on the back of it and shone his light down her throat.

'And again,' he said.

'Ahhhh.'

'Good.' He removed the stick and between his thumb and the palm of his hand, he snapped the stick in two and dropped it into the waste bin. He wrote a note in his book and patted her on the head.

'Okay, my little escapee, you're fine! Back to your class.'

Cathy hopped off the chair and made for the door. She placed her hand on the door handle and stopped. She turned, still holding the handle and said, 'Doctor?' He had his back to her, but turned, 'Yes?' With her left hand she brushed back her fringe and said, 'Thanks!' He smiled, 'My pleasure . . . and hey, nice knickers!'

Cathy giggled and left the room. She went to the cloakroom to dress. She had not been back to her classroom since the big break, as she and the other four girls had come straight to the doctor. As she dressed she reflected on how things had worked out so well and that life was indeed worth living! What she did not know was that after break, when Cathy's cousin Ann did not see her return, she got scared. As soon as the class was seated Ann timidly raised her hand and when Sister Magdalen asked what was the matter, Ann tearfully confessed all. The cat was well and truly out of the bag! As Cathy entered the classroom she noticed a definite air of impending disaster. She did not, however, suspect that this had anything to do with her. She took her seat. Sister Magdalen said nothing to her, but carried on with the English lesson that was in progress.

All was normal for the time being, although Cathy noticed a few peculiar looks from classmates.

The bell rang through the corridors to end the day's schooling, and Sister Magdalen issued her instructions: 'Don't forget questions sixty-five to seventy tonight, we'll be doing them first thing in the morning. Oh, and Miss Browne, you stay after school, I wish to speak to you.'

The class stood and said the 'Hail Mary' aloud. Only the girl standing next to Cathy Browne heard the tremor in her voice. The classroom was soon empty and deathly quiet. Cathy sat alone at her desk. Sister

Magdalen had, as usual, walked her girls down to the front door in single file and would return at any moment. Cathy heard the 'clack, clack' of Sister Magdalen's heels coming towards the room, and the fear tasted like a rusty nail in her mouth. The nun entered. She closed the door and walked to her desk. She did not look at Cathy. Instead she opened the top drawer of her desk. In this drawer was a Bible, a roll-book, used to mark the daily attendance of the each pupil — a dash for present and a circle for absent — a box of blackboard chalk and the 'wrath of God'. The 'wrath of God' was a strip of leather one and a half inches wide, one half-inch thick and twelve inches long. Somebody, somewhere had sat over a drawing board and designed this strip specifically for beating children. It served no other purpose. It was expensive to make and to buy. The nun did not take it out. Instead, she placed her hand on it in the drawer. She still did not look at Cathy. Her eyes were firmly on the 'wrath of God'. She took a deep breath and as she exhaled, she said,

'Miss Browne, do I like lies?'

'No, Sister Magdalen.' Cathy knew what the nun was holding.

'And do I like liars?' The nun still did not look up.

'No, Sister Magdalen.' A tear shot down Cathy's cheek.

'Come up here,' the nun said as she whipped out the strap and slammed it on the desk. Cathy walked unsteadily to the front of the room. The nun was glaring at her now.

'What do liars get?' she asked in a low, husky voice.

Cathy bowed her head and mumbled.

'Speak up, girl!' the nun screamed.

Cathy jumped with fright. The tears were now streaming down her cheeks and dripping from her quivering chin. Her long fringe was damp and stuck to her cheeks.

'The "wrath of God",' Cathy cried.

'The "wrath of God",' the nun repeated, 'so do not lie to me here,' she pointed to the crucifix, 'before God our Saviour.' The nun now seemed to be shaking as much as

Cathy. 'Hold out your hand,' she said as if telling Cathy to sharpen her pencil. The child stretched out her hand and bent her fingers back so that her palm was sticking up. She closed her eyes.

'Why did you leave the school grounds today?'

The question was simple, the answer embarrassing. Cathy was afraid to lie before 'God the Saviour', yet she could not tell the truth, it just wouldn't come out. Whack! The pain shot up her arm and out through her head. Her hand was tingling.

'I am waiting for an answer, Madam,' the nun said and raised her arm again.

Cathy opened one eye. The huge, dark figure loomed over her, the arm pointing to Heaven, the strap flapping like a wild animal's tongue. Cathy withdrew her arm and ran to the door. The nun was startled, but quick enough to catch Cathy before the door was opened. Cathy had now balled her hands into two fists and had them under her armpits. The nun gripped her above the elbow and dragged the girl easily along the polished floor to the desk. She threw the strap on the ground and, still holding the child's arm, rummaged with her free hand in the drawer.

'I'll teach you, Miss . . . Miss . . . trollop!' she said as her hand came out of the drawer clutching a chrome scissors.

By the time Cathy reached home her tears had stopped. As she entered the noisy flat, Agnes said, 'Cathy, your dinner is in the pot, do your homework before you eat it. Where did you get that bloody thing?' Agnes was pointing at the woolly hat with a tassel that Cathy was wearing. It was called a 'monkey hat', after Mike Nesmith, one of the band The Monkees, Cathy's favourite band.

'Ann Reddin gev' it to me.'

'Well, it looks stupid,' Agnes said. But knowing that kids will be kids, she did not interfere with their fashion whims. 'I'm goin' down to Marion. You be in your bed when I get home.'

Cathy went to her bedroom and cried.

Chapter 10

WEDNESDAY MORNING CAME, Marion's day for the doctor. Agnes stood beside the two prams at the bottom of the church steps. As usual, Marion was doing her early-morning shout, except this time, when the echo of 'Good morning, God, it's me, Marion' died down, Marion said softly, 'Don't leave me in trouble today.' As she came back down the steps, Agnes simply said to her: 'All right?', to which Marion answered, 'All right!', and off they went to ply their wares. The morning was busy so the time flew by. Before Marion knew it, Agnes was standing beside her, waiting to leave for Dr Clegg's clinic.

'Are you right?' Agnes asked.

'Nearly. I've only half me apples washed, me mind is not me own.'

'Leave them. Fat Annie will do them for yeh. Come on, it's nearly eleven. Get your coat.'

Marion did, and the women set off on the

fifteen-minute walk to the doctor's clinic rooms. They walked to the end of Moore Street and took a right down Parnell Street towards Summerhill, where Dr Clegg sat each morning from eleven to one. There was no conversation between the women before they reached the huge triangular edifice that was the Parnell monument at the northern end of O'Connell Street. As they passed beneath the giant outstretched hand of Charles Stewart Parnell, Agnes said: 'Did I tell you that my Mark is gettin' pubic hair?'

'Where, on his willy?'

'No, on his tongue! Of course on his willy!'

'How do you know?'

'He told me. Very worried he was. Thought he was abnormal — reformed or somethin'.'

'Ah, God love him. Did he ask you about the "birds and the bees"?'

'No, not really.'

'What do you mean, not really?'

'Well, he asked me why he was getting hair on his willy.'

'What did yeh tell him?'

'I told him it was to keep his willy warm when he's swimmin'.'

The women roared laughing as they stepped on to Gardiner Street and a car screeched to a halt, its horn honking loudly.

'Ah, keep yer horn for someone what loves yeh,' screamed Agnes.

The driver gave her a two-finger salute and drove on. Both women returned the gesture.

'Bleedin' cars, think they own the road,' Marion said as a token of support to Agnes's outburst.

Just one hundred yards up Summerhill and they were outside Dr Clegg's clinic.

'Jaysus, Agnes, I'm shittin' meself.'

'Ah, you'll be grand. Come on, in yeh go — you'll see!' The women hugged each other and entered the clinic.

That evening at six o'clock the Browne children sat or stood around the kitchen awaiting their tea. They chattered amongst themselves while Agnes busied herself at the cooker. She was distracted, and was doing things 'arseways'. She poured the boiling water into the pot but forgot to put tea-leaves in it; she had put bread under the grill to toast it but never turned the grill on. She kept remembering the look of pure terror on Marion's face as she said: 'He wants me to go in for tests next week in the Richmond Hospital.' Marion had burst into tears. They didn't go straight back to Moore Street like they had promised Fat Annie they would, instead they stopped at the pub on the corner and had a drink. Dr Clegg had told Marion that it might be a malignant tumour and if it were, she would have to have a breast removed. Marion was frantic.

'That's only the start, Aggie! First a breast, then a leg, then another leg — bit by bit — and then they bury the bits that are left.'

Agnes slapped her on the face and did some hard talking. 'Listen you, you're 'way ahead of yourself! It could turn out to be nothing. And so what if they take a breast — look at Mona Sweeney in the pawn shop, she has only one diddy and she's grand! Now get a grip.' They had finished the drinks in silence and made their way back to their stalls, and a very irate Fat Annie.

The chattering of the children was rising to a screeching match.

'Shut up!' Agnes screamed. 'All of yis, shut up. This is not the Phoenix Park. If yis have to talk, talk quietly, yis are drivin' me round the fuckin' bend.' All went quiet for a moment, then Cathy spoke up. 'It's Dermo, Ma, he's makin' Marko mad.'

'It's not me, it's him,' Dermo said, pointing at Mark.

'Shut up, I told yis, and Cathy, your brother's names are Dermot and Mark, keep those nicknames for the street.' Agnes put the pot of tea on the table and a huge plate of hot, buttered toast. She wiped her hands on her apron and took it off.

'Mark,' she ordered, 'pour out the tea, and there's two slices of toast for everyone. I don't want to hear any arguing.'

She left the room and bolted herself in the toilet. Peace and quiet. Mark poured out the tea and the toast was seized upon. Dermot started up again, but this time in a quieter voice. 'She's a slut,' he said with an impish grin on his face.

Cathy was next. 'She is not. Maggie O'Brien is very nice, and if Mark loves her that's his own business.'

'Shut up, you don't know anything, you're a kid!' Dermot said with some authority. 'Anyone will tell you, that for a penny worth of liquorice Maggie O'Brien will let you see her bum.' Dermot knew these things.

Mark finished pouring out the tea and with a smile, said to Dermot: 'Well, I'm meeting her at the back of Foley's — and I won't need *any* liquorice.'

The whole crowd of them went 'Wooooo!!'

Dermot was not convinced. 'Why not?'

' 'Cause I have something the other fellas haven't got.'

Dermot thought for a moment. 'You mean hair on your willy?' He laughed — and so did the entire gang except Mark.

'No — charm!' Mark spat out defiantly.

Agnes returned and all went quiet. She poured herself out a cup of tea, sugared and milked it, and leaned against the sideboard.

'Right youse, finish that tea, and into your pyjamas.'

'I have to go out,' said Mark.

'Where?' Agnes spoke like a barrister.

'To the . . . boxing club.'

'Of a Wednesday night? Why, what's on?'

'Eh . . . some man is coming down to talk to us about . . . something.'

'Oh all right, but you be back here by nine, d'yeh hear me?'

'Yeh! Nine!' Mark answered, relieved that his date with Maggie O'Brien — his date with destiny — was allowed to take place. The other children kept their eyes down. Brownes don't snitch.

As Mark skipped down to Foley's, his excitement almost made him burst. So this is love, he thought. He had practised some romantic lines he had heard at the matinees, and was ready to tackle the serious business of wooing his lady. As he rounded the turn from James Larkin Court into James Larkin Street, he saw her standing there outside Foley's pub. His heart leapt. He had never

felt like this about anyone or anything before. He slowed his walk to try and look
'cool'. It was impossible. Cool, me hole, he
thought, and began to run. When he got to
her, she went all coy.

'How ye?' he said.

'How ye,' she answered, without looking
at him.

There was an awkward silence. She was
leaning with her back resting against the
lamp post, and for some reason she kept
slipping her heel in and out of the black
brogues she wore. She's gorgeous, he
thought. Okay, so one of her teeth sticks
out, the one beside the yellow one, but it
was nice in a kinda way. Time for one of his
romantic lines.

He cleared his throat. 'Your hair shines in
the moonlight.'

'Fuck off! Yours isn't even combed!'

Her retort caught him off guard. I must have
said it wrong, he thought. Try another one, his
brain screamed, try another one. 'Your pools
are like big eyes,' he stumbled out.

'What boobs? I haven't got any yet, and if

I had you wouldn't be gettin' your fuckin' hands on them.'

This wasn't going according to plan at all. Say nothing.

'Do you want a kiss or what?' she asked him.

'Yeh,' he answered without hesitation.

'Well not here — go 'round the back,' she said with a shrug of her shoulders.

'Okay.' Mark was now prepared to do anything he was told. He went around the back of Foley's pub. Passing under the toilet window, he heard a cough, and then a fart, and a cigarette butt narrowly missed him as it flew from the window. He climbed as quietly as he could over some beer crates and stopped, looking left and right. He had never been around here before.

'Go right,' she ordered. She *had* been here before. He went right until he came to a corner. It was damp, and enough light spilled from the pub for him to see he was at some kind of back gate. He stopped and turned. She walked up to him and stood before him with her eyes closed. He looked at her in wonder.

She opened her eyes. 'Are *you* all right? Kiss me!' She closed them again.

Mark Browne was about to have his first kiss. He moved right up to her until his nose touched hers, and pushed his face hard against hers. Their lips met, their noses squashed and it lasted all of three seconds. When he pulled away, Mark saw stars before his eyes.

This is great, he thought. Then he thought, I *must* see this girl's bum.

'Wait here,' she said.

'Why? Where are you going?'

'I have to do me pee, wait here!' She vanished around the side of the building. Mark was thinking to himself, I'm never going to see it, when the door he was standing beside began to open slowly and quietly. He froze, terrified. It was Dermo.

'What the fuck . . . ?' he barked, annoyed.

'Here,' Dermo said and disappeared. It was a stick of liquorice.

Mark smiled, and to the now closed door he whispered, 'Thanks, Dermo.'

Chapter 11

THERE IS NO SUCH THING AS A SECRET in Moore Street. Within days, news of Marion's visit to the clinic and the doctor's request for her to go into hospital for tests was all over the markets. There was a path worn to Marion's stall by other dealers who had a solution for her illness, or a story of someone they knew with a similar complaint to Marion's that turned out to be nothing. Fat Annie suggested that it might be an ingrown boil and some time was spent by the other dealers discussing how best to get a poultice on the inside. Doreen Dowdall said it could be an extra nipple, for in a James Bond movie she had seen a man with three nipples and Doreen was convinced it was quite common. Mrs Robinson said one of her twin daughters Splish, or was it Splash?, had had a lump on her breast and it turned out to be nothing more than a cyst.

'It's simple,' she said. 'All they do is lance it.'

Bridie Barnes asked: 'Does that mean that a fella in a suit of armour runs at it with a spear?' All the 'girls' laughed, including Marion.

In general, Marion's problem was treated as a simple matter and nobody really worried about it — except Marion. Agnes had convinced herself that it would turn out to be nothing and that Marion would soon be back to her old self, once the tests were done and the results were in.

Agnes decided she herself needed a lift and planned to concentrate on home for a while and get the front room papered and decorated. The opportunity of doing a bit of work in the house perked Agnes up. There's something about a newly decorated room that puts a woman in good form, she said to herself.

Over the next few days the weather picked up and the Moore Street market was starting to buzz with life again. Agnes found herself in as good a humour as she had been in a long time. So, it was indeed with a light heart that she went to visit Marion in the Richmond Hospital. Marion had been admitted that morning for her tests. Within just three hours of her admission Marion was sitting up in bed, tests completed and just twenty-four hours of bed rest ahead of her. Agnes had knocked into Tommo at teatime that day and Tommo had assured Agnes that Marion was ready for visitors. After feeding her family, Agnes put on a bit of make-up and headed for the Richmond, just fifteen minutes' walk away.

'Monks — Marion Monks,' Agnes said to the porter at the reception desk in the hospital. He flicked through some file pages, and ran his finger down a list until the requested name appeared under his nicotine-stained finger.

'Monks. Mrs Marion. St Catherine's ward,' he announced.

'Where's that?'

'Through the door, take a right, half-way down the corridor take a left, two flights of stairs up, then straight in. Second door on your left.'

Twenty minutes later and after a grand tour of the hospital, Agnes eventually found the ward. St Catherine's ward was a narrow room about ninety feet long.

There were ten beds along by the two longer walls, each with an identical iron bedstead, and each partnering identical steel bedside lockers. The beds were separated by curtain dividers which, when Agnes entered, had been pulled back to allow the patients to see the visitors as they entered. Agnes stood inside the doorway and scanned the beds down along the left-hand wall, and the faces of the patients now staring back at her. No sign of Marion. She felt uncomfortable standing there, on show. She turned quickly and repeated the procedure along the right-hand side of the room and, five beds down, she saw Marion waving furiously.

'Agnes! Agnes! Over here, love,' Marion called.

Quickly Agnes moved towards Marion's bed, removing her headscarf and running her fingers through her hair as she went. She put the obligatory bottle of Lucozade and packet of ten cigarettes on the bedside locker and gave Marion a big hug.

'Sit down! Sit down,' said Marion.

Agnes duly sat and pulled the chair a little closer to the bed.

'Well, how are yeh?' Agnes asked, full of concern.

'I'm grand! No pain, no uncomfortable feelings! Really, I'm grand.' Marion spoke with a smile and Agnes relaxed. As with all hospital visits first things come first. Then Marion pointed to each patient in the ward and described their illnesses in detail, what their visitors were like and what their bad habits were. It seemed that everyone else in the ward, except Marion of course, was a little bit mentally disturbed. Agnes was not surprised that after only a few hours in the ward, Marion had already gathered full case histories on her ward mates. That was Marion. Eventually the conversation turned to Marion's case again.

'Marion . . .' Agnes began hesitantly.

'What?' Marion knew there was a hard question coming.

'What did they do to yeh?'

'Oh now,' began Marion with authority, as if she had that day begun medical school rather than been a patient. 'They done a lumpectomy and a cervical by-hopicy. Then they test them bits, and they find out what's wrong with me!'

Agnes was leaning with one elbow on the bed and her hand tucked under her chin, marvelling at Marion's grasp of the medical details.

'Well, you look marvellous, Marion, really marvellous. I think they cured yeh!'

'Ah no, they haven't even started yet. These are just tests to find out what's wrong with me, *then* they'll cure me.'

'Ooh! I see!' Agnes answered.

Suddenly Marion leaned towards Agnes and spoke in a half-whisper. 'Do yeh know what they done to me?'

Agnes pulled her chair even closer to the bed. 'What?'

'They shaved me!'

Agnes sat back a little and stared at Marion's face. The hairs were still on the moles so they hadn't shaved her chin. Agnes was puzzled. 'They *shaved* yeh! Where?'

Marion glanced around the ward, coughed and patted herself just below the stomach, at the same time tilting her head sideways.

For a moment Agnes still looked puzzled. Then a look of realisation came across her face. 'What? DOWN THERE!' Agnes yelped.

A few visitors' heads turned towards Marion's bed and some of the patients leaned forward to see what was going on. Marion's face turned crimson. She nodded politely, smiled at all and sundry, and then through her teeth to Agnes she said, 'Agnes, for fuck's sake!'

'Oh! I'm sorry, Marion.' She added in a lower tone, 'I don't believe yeh.'

Marion just nodded her head in an exaggerated fashion and said, 'Yep! Shaved me they did! Baldy!'

'Say yeh swear.'

'I swear.'

'Well, my God!' Agnes was open-mouthed.

Now both women glanced around the ward as if expecting spies. For a few moments nothing was said, then Agnes prodded Marion in the side and said, 'Marion, give us a look!'

'I certainly will not!'

'Ah, go on! Give us a look!'

'NO!'

'Marion Monks. I'm your friend. Now, give us a look.' Marion glanced around the ward. 'Pull around the curtain,' she said.

With a swish the curtain went swiftly around the bed so the other visitors could see nothing. But they could hear, and what they heard was Agnes's voice as she exclaimed: 'Ooh! Oh my God! D'yeh know what, Marion? It suits yeh!' And the two women howled with laughter.

Agnes left the hospital in an even happier mood than when she had entered it. Marion was in good spirits. She seemed to be well and there didn't seem to be anything to worry about on that front. With a pep in her step, Agnes Browne was going home to her newly-decorated room, where she would make herself a cup of tea and listen to the sweet sound of her children sleeping.

Chapter 12

AGNES WAITED IN THE EARLY-MORNING sunshine by her stall for Cathy to arrive and collect her lunch. She was in a daze. She stared over at Marion's empty stall space with a heavy heart. It was a week now since Marion had gone into hospital, and she still was not back.

It had been late, after twelve the previous night when Agnes finally left Marion's place for home. Tommo had walked Agnes back to her flat in Larkin Court. Agnes thought nothing of Tommo's offer to walk her home. Little did she know he had a reason for it — he wanted to talk to Agnes out of Marion's earshot. As they strolled down George's Hill in the bright moonlight, Agnes was nattering away about how well Marion was looking and how she knew it would be nothing to worry about. Suddenly Tommo stopped in his tracks. Agnes had walked on a bit before she realised Tommo was not by her side. When it dawned on her, she too stopped, and turned to look back at him. Tommo stood, his head bowed and his huge form shuddering as he sobbed audibly. Agnes was taken aback.

'What's wrong with you, Tommo?' she asked.

'She . . . she's not well, Agnes . . . she's not well at all.'

'Well, of course she's not well, Tommo! Any surgery, even minor surgery, take's a lot out of yeh . . . And you may as well get used to it, 'cause if they have to take the breast . . . she'll be feeling down for a good long while!' Agnes spoke with authority in the hope that she could lift Tommo's spirits. She didn't. He sobbed louder now and was gasping for breath. So much so that he tried, but was unable to speak.

'Ah Tommo, you'll have to get a grip on yourself.' Agnes was now standing hands-on-hips. Tommo just sobbed on.

Agnes opened her handbag and rooted out her cigarettes. She lit one hurriedly. The smoke from the first draw wafted upwards towards the smiling moon. She dropped the pack back into her bag and clipped it shut. Tommo's sobs were less frantic now and he was breathing deeply. A young couple linking arms passed them, the young girl recognising Agnes.

'Good night, Mrs Browne,' the girl said.

Agnes smiled at her. 'Eh . . . yeh, good night, love. Straight home with yeh now!'

The couple chuckled and strolled on. Agnes smiled after them, then turned with a more serious face to Tommo, and spoke in a hushed but firm tone. 'Will you cop on, Tommo. Standin' there sobbin' like a big fuckin' sissy! Anyone would think it was the end of the world!'

'It is . . . for me, Agnes,' he replied, his voice now deeper after his massive flow of tears.

'Why? What's the story?' Even as she asked the question Agnes knew and dreaded the answer. Her body prepared for it, her knuckles going white around the handbag strap, her chest tightening, and her toes curling up as if to try and keep her feet firmly on the ground. Tommo looked her into the eyes, and spoke just two words.

'Six months.'

As Agnes now stared into the space that was Marion's empty stall spot on this sunny morning, those two words echoed in her head.

'Ma! Mammy!' A little voice pierced her stupor and she jumped, startled. It was Cathy.

'What the feck do you want?' Agnes snapped.

'Me lunch.' Cathy's reply was quiet and puzzled.

Agnes bent and hugged her. 'I'm sorry, pet . . . I got a fright. I was miles away . . . I'm sorry . . .'

Agnes let the child out of the tighter-than-usual hug but held on to her shoulders. She smiled into Cathy's face.

'You look lovely, chicken, except for that bloody woolly hat!' and with that she pulled the hat off the child's head. Cathy tried to pull it back on but it was too late. Her mother saw the damage. Agnes said nothing for a few seconds, she just stared at the child

135

open-mouthed. Cathy hung her head.

'Where's your fringe?' Agnes asked. The question came out as if the child had mislaid it.

'Gone,' Cathy answered without looking up.

'I can see it's gone, I'm not Ray fuckin' Charles. Where's it gone? How'd it go?'

Agnes's voice was getting angry.

'Me sister cut it off.'

'You haven't *got* a sister . . . unless you count Rory . . .'

'No . . . me teacher sister . . . Sister Magdalen, she cut it off!' Tears now welled up in Cathy's eyes.

'Why?' Agnes said with agony in her voice. She too now had a watery gaze.

' 'Cause I was bold!' It was all too much for Cathy, she broke into tears. Agnes hugged her only daughter tightly. She used the traditional cure, tapping Cathy's back and whispering in her ear, 'There, there, there!'

When she calmed down, Cathy recounted the whole story to her mother. When Cathy had finished, Agnes smiled at her. 'Not to worry, love. Listen, next Saturday you an' me will go into the hairdresser's and get a style put in that head of yours that would make Lulu jealous. All right, love?'

Cathy threw herself into her Mammy's arms and squeezed her tightly. Very quietly she said, 'I love you, Mammy.'

Agnes again tapped her back and said, 'I know, love, I know. Now, off to school with yeh.'

Cathy stuffed her sandwich and fruit into her bag and trotted merrily up the street. The whole incident had upset her terribly and she was glad it was all over.

But it wasn't!

The morning passed quickly for Agnes. The early trade was brisk and she moved a fair bit of stuff. Marion crossed her mind many times, but Agnes just worked on. At twelve o'clock she walked over to Smelly Nelly, the fish monger, for a smoke and a chat. She didn't enjoy it. Try as she might, she had too much on her mind. When she finished her smoke she went over to Fat Annie.

'Annie, would you keep an eye on me gear

for about a half an hour?'

'Ah Jaysus, Agnes, I was goin' to ask you to mind mine. Me Ma's havin' Father Egan over for tea and I promised her I'd drop her up the makin's of a sambwich.'

Agnes was perturbed, but only for a moment. 'I'll tell you what. Give me yer Ma's stuff and I'll drop it in to her on the way back from the school. Please, Annie, I have to go up there.'

Fat Annie thought for a couple of seconds. 'All right.' She handed Agnes a bag. 'There's corned beef, ham, sala', onions and two cucumbers in there, tell her. And if that's not good enough for Father Egan he should get himself a parish on the southside!'

The two women laughed. Agnes took the bag and headed for the Mother of Divine Providence School.

There are certain smells you remember all of your life. The hospital, a confession box, a pub first thing in the morning. These are all recognisable smells. They cannot be confused with anything else. And you never forget the smell of school, Agnes thought, as she walked the corridor, the echo of her footsteps her only company. She glanced from side to side at each door. She stopped outside room four. Agnes had no idea what she was going to say or do, she just knew she had to come here. Her handbag was in her left hand and the bag Fat Annie had given her was in her right, so to knock on the door Agnes put both bags into her left hand. She rapped on the door. It was opened by a tall nun. Taller than Agnes. For a moment Agnes could picture this big lump of a woman holding down her tiny ten-year-old daughter.

'Yes, Madam?' She sounded like a man.

Agnes just stared at her. She could feel her heart beat louder. Over the nun's shoulder she could see the children looking at her. She couldn't see Cathy. Maybe this was the wrong class.

'Can I help you, Madam?' The nun's tone was now a little irritated.

'I'm looking for Sister Magdalen,' Agnes said flatly.

'I am Sister Magdalen.'

'Well, *I* am Mrs Browne. Cathy Browne's mother.'

'Yes?'

'Who gave you permission to cut her hair?'

'Permission? *Permission?* Mrs Browne, *I* do not *need* permission to keep discipline in my school. Is there anything else?'

Agnes cannot remember putting her hand in the bag — the thing seemed to have just grown out of her palm. One second her hand was empty, next she was wielding a bright green cucumber! She swung it in an arc, catching the nun square across the cheek with it.

Unfortunately for Sister Magdalen the cucumber wasn't quite ripe. Agnes remembers seeing something shoot out of the nun's mouth at the same time as the slap sounded. It was a palate. On which were seven false teeth. The palate clicked across the classroom floor like seven little white tap dancers. Agnes turned on her heel and left the nun lying in the doorway. Half-way down the hallway and without looking back, Agnes shouted: 'Put that in your fuckin' pipe and smoke it!'

The Gardaí were waiting for Agnes at her stall when she returned. She had time only to ask Smelly Nelly to call in and check that the kids would be okay. The two Guards then arrested her and took her to Store Street Garda Station, where she was put into a holding cell to await her court appearance the next day. Looking back, Agnes was thankful for that twenty hours alone in a cell with just her thoughts. For, after mulling over Marion's illness for a long time and thinking about how she should react to it, she came to a decision. She would not refer to it at all. Agnes decided she would spend whatever time she had left with Marion just enjoying her, making her laugh, and above all making the most of every second they had left together. That was one problem solved. Now for the court case.

Agnes was escorted from the 'Paddy wagon' to the court's underground cells. They searched her — probably looking for dangerous fruit or vegetables. When she emerged from the basement cells to the dock there was a cheer from the gallery. Agnes looked up —

there was Fat Annie, Smelly Nelly, Winnie the Mackerel, Liam the Sweeper, Sweaty Betty, Doreen, Catherine, Sandra, Jacko, Splish and Splash, Buddha, her children — and Marion! She waved, and they waved and cheered. The justice banged his gavel.

'Quiet, up there, or I'll have you all thrown out. This is a court of law, not a circus!'

The room went quiet. The justice peered over his glasses, and, satisfied with the quiet, turned to Mrs Browne: 'Agnes Loretta Browne, you are charged with assault with a . . . I'm sorry,' he now addressed the clerk, 'this looks like . . . *cucumber.*'

The clerk reddened and nodded. 'Yes, Justice, it is indeed a . . . er . . . cucumber.'

The justice looked puzzled at first, then he smiled and continued, '. . . with a cucumber, causing actual bodily harm. How do you plead?'

'How do I what?' Agnes asked.

'How do you plead, woman?' the justice snapped.

'Well, I kinda' squash me face up like this . . .' Agnes squashed up her face and turned the sides of her mouth downwards, '. . . and

I say *ah go on, please . . . go on.*'

The justice stared at Agnes, then looked at the clerk who simply shrugged his shoulders. He then looked back at Agnes. She was still in her pleading pose.

'Stop that!' he yelled. She did. He tried again. 'Madam are you trying to mock this court?'

'No, mister.'

'Justice.'

'Mr Justice.'

'No Mister . . . just Justice.'

'No Mister *Just* Justice.'

Again the justice stared.

The clerk stood up and walked over to Agnes. 'When you talk to him you call him Justice,' he whispered.

Agnes was relieved: 'Oh thank God, 'cause his full name is real long — I'd never remember it. Tell him he can call me Aggie.' The clerk returned to his seat, on the way nodding to the justice that all was now explained.

'Now, Mrs Browne,' the justice said, 'can we begin again?'

'Yes . . . Justice.'

'Good girl. Now, did you or did you not assault Sister . . . eh . . . Magdalen, with a cucumber causing her bodily harm? Yes or no?'

'Yes.'

The justice nodded, but Agnes wasn't finished, '. . . and no!'

'What's that supposed to mean? It's either yes or no.'

'Well I did hit her, but all that happened was her false teeth fell out. Sure, there's no harm in that!'

The justice instructed the clerk to enter a plea of 'guilty' to assault, and 'not guilty' to bodily harm. As this exchange was taking place, Agnes interrupted the justice.

'She cut me daughter's fringe off.'

'I beg your pardon?' asked the justice.

'I said, she cut me daughter's fringe off — the nun, she cut it off.'

'Why did the nun, eh, sister, cut your daughter's fringe?'

' 'Cause she went home to change her knickers.'

'What? Whose knickers? This is all very

confusing!' The justice turned and addressed the arresting Garda. 'Is this, em, Sister Magdalen in the court?'

The Garda stood. 'No, justice, but I do have a sworn statement here.'

'That's all well and good, but I cannot question a statement, and I want the whole story.'

Agnes put her hand up, as if in school, and the justice spotted her. 'You wish to speak, Mrs Browne?'

'Yes. Me daughter is here. She'll tell you the whole story.'

'Right, bring her up.'

Cathy was brought to the witness box by Marion. She sat on the chair with her skinny little legs dangling like a frill on a curtain. To a silent courtroom she told her story. Her tale was punctuated from time to time by 'ooh's and 'aah's from the gallery. At one point in the story even the justice let out a 'Tut,tut!'. When she had finished, the courtroom was a picture to be seen: the justice with his hand over his eyes, the arresting Garda, red-faced with embarrassment, turning left and right to those around him, saying, 'I knew none of this, I swear.'

And in the gallery, Smelly Nelly and Winnie the Mackerel were trying to raise a lynching party.

The justice slowly took his hand from his eyes. He spoke to the arresting Garda. 'Do you wish to question this witness, Garda?'

'Absolutely not, Justice.'

'Good.' He turned to Mrs Browne. 'Mrs Browne, I am dismissing all charges against you. However, I do not wish to see you here again. I can and do understand your anger, but you must act within the law. You should have reported this to the police.'

Agnes laughed. 'Ha! What policeman would arrest a nun on my word as quick as I was arrested on hers?'

There were over twenty Gardaí in the court-room. All of them blushed. The justice was lost for a response. Instead he again addressed the arresting Garda. 'Garda . . . eh . . .'

'Dunne, Justice.'

'Garda Dunne. I would like you to call on this Sister Magdalen and inform her of what was said and done here today.'

'I will, Justice.'

'I'm not finished. I also want you to tell her from me and on behalf of the Gardaí that any and all complaints received from parents concerning the ill treatment of children in her care will be fully investigated!'

'I'll do that, Justice!'

'Mrs Browne.'

'Yes, Justice?'

'Take your family home.'

'Oh thank you, Justice.' There followed a huge cheer from the gallery and a smattering of applause from the solicitors, barristers and assorted criminals awaiting their business with the court. In the midst of all of this nobody saw Cathy stand tippytoe at the justice's rostrum. The justice saw only her big brown eyes and tattered fringe. He leaned forward and asked, 'Yes, Cathy?'

'Can I still make me Confirmation?'

'Yes, Cathy, you can of course make your Confirmation.'

The eyes smiled. 'Thanks, Mister!' and off she ran to her mother.

Chapter 13

AS IT HAPPENED, CATHY'S CONFIRMATION DAY was a great success. By the time the hairdresser was finished with her, Cathy was more than pleased with the outcome. On the day she wore a pink two-piece suit decorated with tiny flowers around the edge of the lapel, a white high-collared blouse and white shoes. Archbishop McQuaid gave her the Sacrament of Confirmation, and to her relief Cathy was not even asked a question. The one-and-a-half-hour ceremony was followed by lunch in Bewley's Café which, as always, was sumptuous. Then began the obligatory visiting of friends and relations. Transport for the day was provided by Ned Brady, a local baker. Ned had an Austin Cambridge and supplied the car, himself as driver and the petrol for five pounds. By the end of the day Cathy had visited twelve aunts and uncles, seven of her mother's friends, including Marion and Tommo, and finally Foley's pub. Agnes and

148

Cathy arrived home at nine o'clock, exhausted. No sooner were they in the door than Cathy began emptying her pockets and handbag of half-crowns, ten-shilling notes, and the odd pound note. Agnes went to her bedroom and took off her 'good' dress and with a huge sigh of relief peeled off the roll-on that had seemed to be shrinking as the day wore on. When she returned to the kitchen Cathy was sitting at the table with her Confirmation money all sorted.

'Well, how'd you do?' Agnes asked her.

'Sixteen pounds and twelve shillings,' Cathy answered with awe in her voice.

'My God, you lucky thing! When I made my Confirmation I got all of eight shillings, and I was delighted.' The battle-cry of all parents.

Cathy just sat and surveyed her money. All this money, more than she had ever seen. Agnes sat down at the table opposite her.

'So, have you decided what you're going to do with it all, love?'

'Yeh,' Cathy answered, pleased with herself.

'So what's it to be?'

'Well, I thought, two shillings each for Dermo, Rory, Simon and Frankie. Half-a-crown for Marko. That's . . . eh . . . ten-and-six right? Then one-and-six to buy Trevor a ball. That leaves sixteen pounds, and I'm keeping a pound for meself!' The child was glowing with the chance of being Santa Claus.

'That still leaves you fifteen pounds, love. Do you want me to save it for you?' Agnes asked.

'No, Mammy — that's for you!'

'For me?' Agnes was taken aback. Fifteen pounds was three weeks' profit from the stall.

'Yeh! for you, Ma! To buy anything you want.'

'Oh you're very good, love, but I couldn't!'

'Mammy, please take it. I want you to have it. Buy some Cliff Richard records with it!'

Agnes laughed. 'With that kinda money I could buy all his records. No, I'll tell you what I'll do with it — I'll put a carpet on the floor! A nice bit of exminister, none of that tintain stuff, real exminister with underfelt and all. Wouldn't that be nice?'

'Lovely, Mammy. Can I go with you when you're buying it?'

'Not only can yeh come, you can pick it!'

Cathy was ecstatic. 'Great!' she screeched, and ran around the table for a hug.

'Shh!' Agnes whispered, 'you'll wake the boys. Go on off to bed, and hang that suit up. I might have to pawn it!' Cathy had started to walk away but turned around, shocked with the mention of the word 'pawn'.

'Only jokin', love,' Agnes laughed. And so did Cathy as she floated into her bedroom.

Agnes was struggling with the go-car down the steps, followed by Cathy holding Trevor. The 'baby' was huge for his age, but unlike all of her other children who had been walking everywhere by their third birthday, Trevor insisted on being either carried or pushed in the go-car. Trevor was also slow to speak. At three Mark was reciting the alphabet, Dermot was telling lies and Cathy could sing you any song. But not Trevor. It wasn't that he was slow, he was just bone lazy. His vocabulary consisted of about thirty words. Agnes suspected that he knew a lot more, but just did not want to use them. His most common phrases were of course the ones you didn't want him to use — things like 'Fuck off', 'Oh shit!' or 'Ask me arse' came out clear as day. He also had, for some reason, decided on obscure names for things and no matter how Agnes tried to teach him the proper names, he stuck steadfastly to his own choices. For instance, 'breakfast' was 'ragga, ragga'. This sounded nothing like breakfast but when Trevor said 'ragga, ragga' he got a cereal. His penis was 'moo moo'! Agnes tried to get him to say 'willy', but no way would he change. At this moment in time Trevor was shouting 'Go day', which meant he knew he was going to be pushed around Dublin in his go-car.

When Agnes reached the bottom of the stairs she took Trevor from Cathy and placed him in the go-car. She fixed the straps around him and then asked Cathy, 'Where's the rope?' The rope was used along with the straps. Because Trevor had mastered the art of unclipping the straps, Agnes now also tied him into the go-car. The rope was tied around one ankle, brought around the side bar, across his chest, around the back of the go-car, back across his chest, around the side bar on the opposite side and finally tied to the other ankle. The neighbours called the child 'Houdini'.

Just as Agnes, Cathy and go-car were about to exit onto the street in walked Mrs Ward. She beamed at the trio.

'Good morning, Mrs Browne,' she said.

'Good morning, Mrs Ward.'

'Hello, Cathy.'

'Hello, Mrs Ward.'

'Ah . . . and hello, little Trevor!'

'Fuck off,' answered Trevor with a smile, and with that the trio were out in the street.

Today was the day that the new carpet was to be chosen. Agnes headed down James Larkin Street towards the city. About one-third of the way down the street she noticed that there were builders working on a shopfront across the road from Foley's pub.

'What's that goin' on?' she asked Cathy.

'It's a new chipper.'

'A chipper? Sure we already have Macari's! What do we want with another one?'

'No, it's not that kinda one, Ma! It's goin' to sell pizzas.'

'What are they?'

'I dunno, but Cathy Dowdall says they're lovely.'

'Are they foreign?'

'Must be.'

'Well, the Brownes won't be eatin' anythin' foreign, so they can keep it!'

They were now abreast of the new shop and Agnes glanced in the window. What made her stop was the carpet. She had never seen carpet in a chipper, for a start, and on top of this, the carpet on the floor was exactly what she had in mind for the flat. She backed up to look at it properly. A man came out of the shop. He was tanned and handsome and very attractive. He looked at Agnes standing there, her face pressed up against the shop window and at the same time trying to shield the reflection with her hand. He was French, had just arrived in Ireland to help set up his father's pizza parlour and this was his first contact with an Irish woman.

'Whee h'air nut h'open yit, lady,' he tried.

Agnes turned and stared at him. He was really handsome.

'I beg your pardon?'

'I say . . . de place es anot h'open!'

'The place is not open, is that what you're tryin' to say?'

'Yes . . . dis ees it!'

'Do I look like I give a shite?'

'Yes, that's right, we h'open tonight.'

'No, I said shite . . . sh . . . ah it doesn't matter! Look, where did you get that carpet?'

'Sorry, you spik too fast.'

'Too fast? Right. Where . . . did . . . you . . .' Agnes pointed, 'getto . . . that . . . carpet . . . eh . . . carpeto?' Agnes now was on one knee slapping the ground. Another man joined the first one and both looked at Agnes as if she were mad. Agnes tried again, this time to the second man. 'Scuso meo . . . the carpeto . . . which shoppo did you get it in . . . o?'

The second man wrinkled his forehead,

turned his head toward the shop door and yelled, 'Hey, lads! Come out an' look at this wan! She's a looney.'

'You speak English!' Agnes exclaimed.

'I'm from Sheriff Street, love, we nearly *all* do up there.'

'Well, he doesn't.' Agnes pointed at the foreigner.

'Ah, he's French, but he's all right. They got the carpet in McHugh's of Capel Street, love.'

'Ah thanks. It's nice isn't it?'

'Yeh, it is. It's nice, all right.'

'I'll see yeh, thanks.' Agnes took hold of the go-car and pushed on. But the Frenchman grabbed her arm and stopped her.

'Hello! My name ees Pierre,' he smiled.

'Eh, lovely. I'm delighted for yeh.' Agnes went to move on but he wouldn't let go. She looked down at his hand. No wedding ring. He let go.

'What ees *your* name, ladee?'

'My name is Agnes. Agnes Browne.'

'You ees fery beeautiful, Agnes Browne.'

Agnes blushed and pushed away from him.

'You mind your mouth, yeh . . . yeh . . . Frenchman!'

Agnes scurried down the street towards town. Just before she turned the corner she looked back. He was standing where she had left him, one hand in his pocket, and looking after her. He raised his other hand and waved at her. Agnes threw her head back indignantly and went around the corner.

'He's nice looking, Mammy!' Cathy said.

Agnes giggled and said, 'Yeh, he is!'

Buying the carpet was a cinch. They knew exactly what they wanted when they walked in the door of McHugh's. It took all of five minutes. Cathy was a little disappointed, but she said nothing as she could see that Mammy was beaming.

Chapter 14

THE SUMMER BROUGHT A NEW WARMTH to Moore Street, in every sense of the word. It was busier for a start, and the wandering shoppers now strolled up and down the market street with a smile on their faces. The scent of strawberries and freshly picked raspberries hung in the air and the dealers' melodious cries, interspersed with laughter, made Agnes feel good to be alive. No sooner had this thought passed through her mind than she glanced over at Marion and felt strangely guilty.

'Are ye all right, Kaiser?' she yelled across at her.

Marion looked up at the sound of her nickname and when her eyes met with Agnes's they smiled, the tiny grey dots turning to tiny grey slits. 'How could you be all right with all this shite you have to put up with here?' Marion gestured with a wave of her arm to the four shoppers that were picking through the fruit on her stall. Realising she was the target of the gesture, one woman shopper looked up and snorted. Marion snorted back at her.

Yes, you're all right, Marion, thought Agnes.

'Pick me out three nice cooking apples for apple tarts,' the woman ordered Marion.

'Pick yeh out! D'ye want me to peel them as well? Sure, I've nothin' else to do,' Marion replied.

The woman was startled at first, but then seeing the cheeky grin on Marion's face she burst out laughing and Marion joined in. 'Here yeh are, Missus, three of me best and that's ninepence.'

The woman handed over the ninepence and moved on with a beaming smile on her face. Marion looked over at Agnes and gave a little wink.

'I don't know how ye get away with it,' Agnes called.

'Because I'm loveable and cuddly, and me apples is the best,' answered Marion with a laugh.

Agnes smiled to herself Marion's spirits never seemed to flag even though little by little as the days went by Agnes saw her deteriorate.

Since that night in her prison cell Agnes had never mentioned the word 'cancer' to Marion, and Marion could boast likewise. Still Agnes's heart sank a little every day. At first it was Marion's skin colour. It had quite suddenly turned a yellowish tan. Marion explained this by saying, 'Ah it's them bloody drugs I'm on, they have me banjaxed.' Agnes tried to get Marion to stay at home, to leave the stall for a while. 'Until you're right again.' The lie stuck in her throat. But Marion was having none of it. Life went on as usual. Each morning at five o'clock, Marion would be there to meet Agnes and set off for a full day's work. She worked as hard as ever and where at first Agnes would be watching her and worrying about her, eventually Agnes began to relax and just enjoy Marion's company.

'It must be that time,' Agnes called again to Marion.

'Yeh, it is. I'll be over in a minute,' Marion answered. There were only a couple of minutes now to the ritual morning break. They both looked forward to their morning chats. Agnes turned to serve a customer yet another 4lb bag of potatoes. She often felt that her life was made up of nothing but 4lb bags of potatoes. In all walks of life people measured their lives in different ways — well, Agnes Browne measured hers by 4lb bags of potatoes. She made sixpence on a 4lb bag, so if she wanted, say, a dress that cost £2 Agnes would immediately think: that's 80 bags of potatoes I have to sell, and she would wonder was it worth it!

Within minutes Marion had arrived, the crates were upturned, the bovril was poured, the cigarettes lit, and the morning chat begun. It was Marion this morning who made the opening statement.

'I was dead proud of you in that court room, Agnes, you were dead right.'

'I was stupid!'

'Stupid! No, you were right.'

'Nah! Marion, the judge or justice or whatever he was was right. I should have gone to the Guards.'

Marion thought about this, took a sip of her bovril and another drag of her cigarette, then shook her head and said, 'No! If it was my daughter I would have done the same.'

Agnes didn't reply and for a couple of moments the two women glanced around the street. Although to the casual visitor Moore

Street seemed to be a cacophony of voices, the two women could distinguish one from the other, and could easily pick out the response of Winnie the Mackerel when a customer asked if the fish was fresh. 'Fresh!' says Winnie. 'Fresh! I guarantee yeh, Missus, if you bring that home to your fella ye'll be putting him out with the cat tonight.' They could hear Doreen Dowdall at her flower stall and the woman asking, 'Do those flowers come from Holland?' and Doreen saying, 'No, love, bulbs. They come from bulbs.' Even a hundred yards away they could hear the stuttering Robinson sisters as they yelled, 'ripe st . . . st . . . strawberries! Ripe str . . . str . . . strawberries!'

Agnes's gaze was drawn back once again to Marion — her tiny frame always a bundle of energy, never an unkind word to say about anyone, oh yeh, always with a caustic remark but never a bit of harm. Agnes couldn't imagine how she would have managed the first four months of widowhood without Marion by her side. The Browne children all called her Auntie Marion and she loved them as if they were her own.

'Marion,' Agnes asked gently.

'What?'

'D'yeh ever regret not havin' kids — yeh know, more kids.'

'Aw Jaysus, I do. But after Philomena died, I dunno . . . Tommy didn't seem interested. It wasn't for the want of trying, I suppose, but his heart wasn't in it and I suppose mine wasn't either.' Philomena was Marion's first and only child. Since Philomena died Agnes had heard a lot about cot deaths, but up until then she had never heard of it. She recalled the horrible memory of that winter morning eight years ago when Tommo stood at Agnes's door saying, 'Agnes, please come down, Marion can't wake the baby up,' and the pitiful sight of Marion sitting on the edge of the bed and rocking back and forth, humming and going 'Shhhh', and then humming again and then refusing to hand the bundle over to the ambulance men when they came. The memory would live with Agnes all her life.

Marion leaned across and tapped Agnes

on the lap, bringing Agnes out of her reminiscing. 'Sure, I always have yours! God knows, they're a big enough handful for both of us,' and she smiled.

Agnes jumped. 'Jesus, speaking of mine — Mark's off on a camping trip. It's this summer project camp and I'm supposed to get him a tent! Where would I get a tent?' Agnes looked around as if expecting to find one there on the street.

'D'yeh have to get it now?' asked Marion.

'Well, he's going in the morning. Buddha said he would pick me up an ex-army one — no sign of it though. Marion, yeh wouldn't keep an eye . . . I'll go and see if some of the shops have them!'

" 'Course I will,' said Marion. 'Go on, take your time, love!'

Agnes whipped off her apron, said, 'Thanks, Marion,' and disappeared up Moore Street.

As it turned out, it didn't take too long. Agnes was back within half-an-hour smiling from ear to ear. She waved across at Marion. 'I got it! I was told they'd be dear but I got one for only fifteen shillings. Massive! And brand new as well.'

Marion waved back. 'Ah, that's great. Mark'll be delighted.'

The summer project was a great help in keeping the young Brownes out of trouble. It was Father Quinn's idea. He was a young priest who came to the parish six years before and with him he brought a lot of young ideas. It was Father Quinn who started St Jarlath's Boxing Club which Dermot belonged to. It was Father Quinn who got Mrs Shields, the old woman who played the organ in the church, to start up the Sunday afternoon ballroom dancing classes which Cathy went to. And Father Quinn managed the Saturday afternoon schoolboys football team, City Celtic, which Mark played for. Agnes Browne and the community of The Jarro had a lot to thank Father Quinn for. This summer project encompassed a lot of things. There was a sports day for the kids in The Jarro. There were painting mornings for the younger ones, and he even trooped thirty-five children down to the Tara Street baths where they all splashed about for an hour.

The camping trip was to be the final event in the summer project and Father Quinn was looking forward with relish to the three days away, as were the forty children he was to take with him. Agnes was thrilled when she heard Mark say he wanted to go. God knows, he earned the five shillings it cost, she thought. She had been troubled with Mark since Redser's death and now that school was over Mark said he had no intention of going on to technical school and wanted to get himself a job. This upset her because she didn't want Mark to end up as another Redser, but she knew that open confrontation would only make him more determined — after all he was *her* son too. So she had decided that gentle persuasion would be the way to go, and every day or so she'd drop a little hint about how important further schooling was. Mind you, it didn't seem to be working. Mark seemed to be determined. Maybe the few days away camping with Father Quinn would change his mind.

Mark, as usual, was up at first light on the

morning of the camping. He made a beeline for Agnes's bedroom, shaking her gently. 'Ma! Mammy! Ma!'

Agnes stirred a little at first, then slowly turned around to him.

'What love? What! What's up?'

'The tent! Did you get the tent?'

'It's outside on the kitchen table. It's wrapped in brown paper and there's two pieces of twine that you can slip your arms into so it'll be like a haversack.'

Mark liked the sound of that as he didn't have a haversack. He had his swimming trunks and his towel ready, and some hard-boiled eggs, sliced bread and butter wrapped in tinfoil all packed into a plastic carrier bag. He sprinted out to the kitchen table and tried on the brown package.

'Yahoo!' He was delighted. He was like a real camper. He washed and dressed in ten minutes, slipped the brown package on to his back, took his carrier bag with all his stuff and made his way down the stairs towards the assembly point outside St Jarlath's church with the rest of the adventurers. It was a beautiful fresh sunny day and Mark took long strides as he headed for St Jarlath's. He arrived outside the church to complete bedlam. One group of boys were playing football up against the side of the church while another group was fighting over God knows what. Two boys were sitting on the steps of the church taking big slugs of milk from pint bottles they had stolen from a doorstep on the way down.

Father Quinn emerged from the Sacristy and soon knocked some kind of semblance of order into the children. Then he lined them up in two rows and they marched down O'Connell Street like an army. Mark felt like a soldier. At the bottom of O'Connell Street they boarded the Blessington bus, two by two. Father Quinn decided who sat beside whom and despite pleading with Father Quinn, Mark ended up sitting beside 'Number Eleven'. Number Eleven was David Molloy, and he got his name from the continuous stream of mucus that flowed from his nose. He was only called Number Eleven in the summer — in the winter the children called him Bubbles, for obvious reasons. Mark eventually sat where he was told to sit, but he kept a close eye on Number Eleven and every time Eleven leaned to the right, Mark leaned away, as if Eleven had an infectious disease. The trip was two hours long and Mark had to concentrate the whole time.

Father Quinn knew one song only: 'Where Have You Been All Day, Henry, My Son' and the kids joined in with gusto. As they neared Blessington, he began the song for the eighth time and the children groaned. Finally, Father Quinn stood up and when he had got everyone's attention, he began to speak: 'Now, children, we're very nearly there and I will shortly be going around to give everybody sixpence to spend.' This was met with a huge cheer. The priest raised his hand and eventually got silence and continued: 'You may, if you wish, spend this on sweets, but please remember to make these sweets last, for, once we leave Blessington on our hike, we will not see civilisation again for three days.'

Blessington was ill-prepared for what was

about to descend upon it. Although a picturesque little village, Blessington was not a sleepy little village and the residents and traders were well aware of their tourist potential, and although the Main Square or Diamond was dotted only with small shops, they did provide for all the needs of tourists. Across the street from where the bus puffed in was a tiny general store. Each summer morning the shopkeeper would come out early and hang up all his colourful wares on meat-hooks around the doorway. There would be inflatable rings for children going bathing, brightly coloured buckets and spades, footballs of all colours and little windmills on sticks gently twirling in the wind. To anybody else stepping off the bus this shop would be picturesque. To Father Quinn's little army from The Jarro, it was a shoplifter's dream.

Twenty minutes later the troop marched up the mountain path from the village, each boy with his pockets full of sweets, postcards, biscuits, tins of salmon, firelighters and cigarettes. They were led proudly by Father Quinn, while back in the shop the shopkeeper was scratching his head and looking at the five shillings he had managed to drag out of the boys. Four miles into the mountains and three more puffing blasts of 'Where Have You Been All Day, Henry, My Son' from Father Quinn and the group came to a lake. Father Quinn turned to the boys, gestured with his arm proudly, and announced: 'Boys, I have led you to the land of milk and honey.' From somewhere in the group a tiny voice said, 'It looks like fuckin' water to me,' and this was followed by a ripple of laughter.

The group marched into the field, then down to the edge of the lake. Father Quinn gathered the boys around and said: 'Boys, put down your baggage and first things first — everybody must collect wood for the bonfire.' There was a large cheer and the children scattered in every direction. 'Make sure it's dead wood,' Father Quinn called after them and when the wood arrived back in dribs and drabs it was indeed dead — some of it dead so long that it had been turned into a door or picket fence! Two of the boys even arrived back with their wood in a wheelbarrow. When Father Quinn asked where they had got the wheelbarrow, they swore they had found it, just like the boys who brought the door and the fence. Father Quinn couldn't shake off the feeling that they had taken the wheelbarrow from somebody's garden and were able to get it out easily because the picket fence was missing! He was afraid even to imagine where the door had come from.

By eight o'clock that evening the boys started to get tired and Father Quinn decided to let everybody put their tent up. He paced out sites five feet apart and ordered them to begin. Mark gleefully took his brown paper packet and began to undo the tape, while beside him Sean O'Hare was unpacking his. Sean O'Hare's tent was a standard army one-man tent bought in a second-hand shop in Dublin — khaki green with two short poles and a ground sheet. When Mark unfolded his package it had eight poles!

'Sean!' he shouted, 'should a tent have

eight poles?'

'Only if you have four tents,' said O'Hare.

But Mark quickly grasped that the poles slotted into one another and instead of eight poles he had four long ones. Again he turned to O'Hare for advice.

'Sean! I have four poles — is that better?'

'It is if you have two tents,' said O'Hare. 'Take out the tent and open it out, then you'll see how many poles you need.'

Mark opened the second brown bag. The first thing he noticed was the bright orange colour of his tent fabric. As he unfolded the fabric and spread it across the ground the next thing he saw was the red Indian markings that were painted on the outside.

O'Hare scratched his head. 'What the fuck is that?'

'It's me tent,' said Mark.

'Are yeh sure, it's not a frock? O'Hare said and laughed loudly. The bright orange colour of the tent was now attracting attention from boys within a twenty-yard radius and they converged on Mark to see what kind of tent he was erecting. It was Number

Eleven who spotted it first.

'It's a bleedin' wigwam,' he screamed and all the boys laughed.

'Don't be stupid!' said Mark, 'it's me tent!'

'I'm tellin' yeh,' Number Eleven went on, 'it's a bleedin' wigwam, I seen them in the toy shops.'

It took only seconds for Mark to realise that Number Eleven was right. It was indeed a wigwam. Bright orange with Indian paintings all around the sides. Agnes had bought her son a teepee. And so for the three nights they spent in the Wicklow Mountains Mark Browne slept in a sitting position, and got himself the name 'Sitting Bull'. A casual passer-by would look down at the lake and see all the khaki tents laid out in military fashion with a priest marching up and down, and in the middle of them all a bright orange wigwam.

When Mark returned from his three-day adventure his mother's advice was less welcome than it had ever been, and any thoughts she had of stopping him going to work and encouraging him back to school went out the door with the wigwam so t'speak.

Chapter 15

THE OTHER BROWNE KIDS HAD their summer outings too, and thanks to the St Vincent de Paul charity they even managed to get themselves a holiday. They had a two-week stay at the 'Sunshine Home' in Skerries. Not for the first time did Agnes bless the Vincent de Paul.

Agnes herself spent the time without the children with Marion. The two drank, talked, walked, and even took a couple of coach trips down the country. Marion was more full of life than Agnes had ever seen her and they laughed themselves silly. However, when the sun began to set a little earlier, and the scent of summer had got thinner in the air, Marion's enthusiasm began to flag. By mid-autumn she was getting tired more easily. She became the victim of huge mood swings, the brunt of which were borne by an increasingly depressed Tommo. It was, Agnes reflected, as if Marion knew she had just had her last summer. Once again Agnes tried to get Marion to give the stall a break for a while and spend the time at home.

'I'd die at home all day every day,' Marion would say with a wry grin. Agnes wondered if she knew. She suspected that she did, for Marion began to do funny things — things that were out of character. For instance, she now held Tommo's hand — in the pub, out shopping, all the time. And one chilly morning when Marion came over with the bovril for the morning break they had an unusual conversation.

When the fags were lit it was time for the ritual chat, but instead of the usual chatter, Marion opened with a question: 'Have you any dreams, Agnes?'

'Oh Jaysus, I have. I'd love to win the sweepstake and get the fuck outta here.' The two laughed. Then came a pause.

'Ah no, I mean *real* dreams,' Marion asked again.

'Like at night in bed?'

'No . . . How do I mean it? Yeh know, some-

times you feel that life is passin' you by . . .
you're doin' nothin', oh you're busy all right,
but your not *doin'* anythin'. D'ye ever feel that?'

'I haven't a clue what you're bleedin'
talkin' about.'

'Ah yeh know . . .'

'I don't know, Marion, I don't. Busy doin'
nothin' — what the fuck is that supposed to
mean?'

'Cliff Richard!' Marion exclaimed.

'What about him?'

'You told me once that you'd love to
dance with Cliff Richard. Am I right?'

'Yeh.'

'Well, that's what I mean! That's a real
dream. That's something that *could* happen!'

'Oh sure, Marion. Cliff will stroll down
Moore Street to my stall and say: How yeh,
Agnes, give us five red apples and, c'mere,
will yeh dance with us?'

'Could happen. I'm not sure about the apples though!'

The two women laughed again, and Agnes
was relieved that Marion wasn't going off
her rocker. But Marion wasn't finished yet.

'Do you know what I'd like to do before I die?'

Marion said this without looking at Agnes and likewise Agnes looked away, scratched her neck and tried to sound as casual as she possibly could. 'What?'

'I'd love to learn to drive!' Marion answered, excited.

'What? Drive? Drive what?'

'A car, of course!'

'But you haven't got a car.'

'So? People do learn Spanish.'

'What's that got to do with drivin' a car?'

'People learn Spanish and they don't go to Spain, so why shouldn't I learn how to drive?'

Agnes had no answer for this perverted logic. She just sat open-mouthed. Marion took this as a request for more information and went on.

'There's a drivin' school in Talbot Street. I called in, and it costs nine pounds for fifteen lessons. That's a savin' of over two pound, cause it's fifteen shillings a lesson. It's a special pre-Christmas offer. What do yeh think?'

Agnes still did not change her expression.

She was digesting all of this, slowly. She spoke slowly too. 'You're goin' to pay out nine pounds . . . to learn to drive something you haven't got?'

'It's me dream . . .'

'Fuck the dream! Get a cheaper dream. You're out of your mind, Marion, really, it's ridiculous!'

Neither of the two women spoke for a while, well not to each other anyway. Agnes would take a sup of bovril and say, 'Drive, me arse,' to herself, and other than that all was silent. Marion stood and took the mugs, brushed down her apron and screwed the stopper back on the flask. She was just about to leave, but instead she put her hand on Agnes's arm and said: 'If you could dance with Cliff Richard for nine pounds you'd fuckin' jump at it!' And she walked back to her stall.

And it wasn't over. That night after the Bingo, Marion brought up the subject again. The two were on their second round of pints, the post-mortem on the Bingo was finished and as usual both were taking in what was happening at the tables around them.

'There's Dermot Flynn,' Marion pointed out.

'Dermot Flynn? Where?' Agnes strained her neck.

'Over there, at the domino table.'

'Oh I see him. He's lookin' well.'

'Is he happy with his move out of town?'

'I don't know. I haven't seen him since they moved. You can be sure she's happy. She has notions, that wan!'

'Yeh, town wouldn't be good enough for her.' Marion confirmed that Dermot Flynn's wife was a snob.

'Mind you . . .' Marion continued, 'when you can drive you can move where you like.' She took a sip. Agnes saw the bait splashing in the water. She was tempted to change the subject and annoy Marion, but she had already given it some thought. Marion was right, Agnes would pay nine pounds to fulfil her dream and dance with Cliff — she'd pay ninety pounds if she had it! So, if Marion could fulfil her dream, stupid as it was, then why shouldn't she? So she rose to the bait.

'I was thinkin' about that, Marion.'

'About what, Agnes?' Marion was milking it!

'You learnin' to drive, what you said today.'

'Oh yeh! Janey, I forgot about that — what about it?'

'You're right!'

'Am I? D'ye think so, Agnes?' Marion was excited now.

'Yeh, yeh are, do it!'

'Ah I'm delighted you agree with it, Agnes. The man in the school said he could take us out next Tuesday night for the first one!'

'Lovely. Wait a minute! What do yeh mean *us?*'

'Us. You and me. I'm not gettin' into a car with a stranger on me own.'

'Well, I'm not gettin' in with yeh — who'll be drivin'?'

'I will.'

'Yeh can fuck off, Marion Monks, if you think I'm goin' to be your first victim!'

'Ah ye'll be all right, Agnes. The car has controls on his side as well, it's . . . it's bisexual, he can take over any time he likes. You just have to sit in the back — mortal support, that's all!'

'No.'

'Agnes . . . for yer pal.'

'NO, NO, NO!'

'I'll get you a cider. PJ, when you're ready?'

'You can buy all the cider in China, the answer is NO. N.O. — NO!'

Chapter 16

MARION'S TINY GREY EYES SPARKLED with excitement as they gazed from the small, elongated rear-view mirror.

'Are you all right in the back, Agnes?'

'Never mind me, you watch the fuckin' road.' Agnes was terrified. She couldn't believe she'd let Marion talk her into this.

'Agnes, relax for God's sake.' Marion turned around in the driver's seat. 'I'd hate to see you if the car was goin'.'

'Don't touch anything you, d'ye hear me? Wait till yer man comes out. Don't touch anything — oh shite, we're movin'!'

'We are not! Ah, Agnes, will yeh stop! If I'd known you were goin' t'be like this I wouldn't have let you come!'

'*Let* me come? Let me fuckin' come? You dragged me here, yeh bloody bitch.'

Marion saw the driving instructor close the door of the office building and make his way to the car. 'Say nothin', Agnes, here's the constructor!'

Marion sat properly in the car, facing forwards. The instructor walked around the vehicle, clipboard in hand, as if examining the vehicle — and that is exactly what he was doing. The women's heads followed him around the car.

'What's he doin'?' asked Marion.

'Dunno — is he lookin' for a way in?'

'Don't be silly, it's his car! He's probably doin' a safety check.'

'He knows we're from The Jarro, Marion, he's countin' the fuckin' wheels!'

Both women howled with laughter. The instructor stopped and looked at the laughing women. They both stopped abruptly. Marion spoke, trying not to move her lips: 'Oh Suck, he diddle like that!'

Agnes looked closer at the man now. He was completely bald, with a flat nose. She whispered to Marion: 'Jaysus, look at the puss on him, someone hit him with a fryin' pan.'

'Agnes, fuck off! I'll start laughin' again.'

The instructor tapped on Marion's window. Marion looked at him, po-faced.

'What?' she yelled.

The instructor made a fist of his hand and moved it in a circular motion.

'He wants a wank!' said Agnes.

Marion burst out laughing again.

Agnes covered her face with her hands. 'Well, he can fuck off.' And the two howled harder.

The instructor put a hand to his mouth. 'Roll down the window, please,' he yelled.

'What'd he say?' Marion asked Agnes.

'He wants to know if you're a widow,' Agnes replied.

Marion shook her head in exaggerated movements and yelled 'Nooo!'

The instructor looked puzzled. 'Wind the

knob!' He pointed downwards.

'What'd he say?' Marion asked again.

'I'm not sure. Something about his knob — he does want a wank, the pervert!'

'Hang on, I'll open the window, we'll hear him better.'

Marion opened the window and Agnes leaned forward to catch what was being said. Marion smiled. 'I couldn't hear you with the window up,' she explained.

'That's what I was . . . oh never mind. I just want to check the brake lights. Press on the brake pedal.'

Marion looked down at the pedals. She lifted her foot and pressed it down on one of the pedals. The instructor shook his head.

'No, no, Mrs Monks, that's the accelerator. We mustn't get these two mixed up. The brake pedal stops the car, the one you are pushing makes it go faster!'

Agnes jumped up and tried to crawl between the two front seats. 'I'm gettin' out! Fuck this!'

Marion pushed her back. 'Will you relax, Agnes. I'm only learnin'. Now!' she declared as she pushed her foot down on the brake pedal.

'That's it,' exclaimed the instructor and he walked to the back of the car to check that both lights were working. Marion watched him in the mirror, Agnes turned to see him bathed in red light, and Marion spoke to the back of Agnes's head. 'Will you relax! What'll he think of us?'

The instructor made a note on his clipboard and put his pen away.

'Ah shut up! Who cares what he thinks? He looks like a big penis!' The women giggled.

'Shh . . . he's comin',' said Marion.

'Ask him his name. I bet it's Mickey! I bettcha!!'

The passenger door opened, and the instructor sat into the seat. He slammed the door shut. 'Right, Mrs Monks, let's begin.'

'Please call me Marion.'

'Okay, Marion . . .'

'What's your name?' Marion asked. Both women waited expectantly.

'Oh I'm sorry.' He put his hand out. 'Tom.' He smiled.

'Oh?' Marion said, disappointed.

'Tom O'Toole,' he finished.

The women burst into hysterical laughter. Tears flowed from Agnes's eyes and her cheeks were streaked with mascara. Marion gripped her stomach with both hands and bent forward until her forehead touched the steering wheel. Agnes fell back and rolled from side to side in the back seat. The instructor was startled at first but as the laughter continued he became very irate.

'Ladies . . . please!'

It took a little time, but the two women eventually stopped . . . for the moment. The women were now infected with the dreaded giggles. For the present, though, they were quiet.

The instructor began: 'Now, turn the key and push the accelerator gently.'

Marion did this, and the engine gunned into life.

'That's good. Now, depress the clutch.'

'What?' Marion asked.

'Depress the clutch.'

'How do I do that?' asked Marion, but before the instructor could answer, Agnes was in with: 'Show it your electricity bill!' The women were off again, howling and slapping the seats. Suddenly Marion stopped and slumped forward. Agnes carried on laughing a little longer, but then noticed that Marion was not moving. She prodded Marion's back and still with a laugh in her voice said, 'Hey, Kaiser!' Marion did not move. Agnes jumped up and out of the car. She ran to the driver's door and pulled it open. Marion had started to come round.

'What's wrong?' Marion mumbled.

'Are you okay? Oh Marion, love, are you okay?'

'I . . . I think so . . . but I feel tired . . .'

'Has she been drinking?' the instructor asked accusingly.

Agnes ignored him, helped Marion gently out of the car, and stood her against the passenger door. Marion looked deathly white, even her lips had paled. She was shaking. Agnes wanted to do something, anything, to help Marion, but she could think of nothing, to either do or say, so she took Marion in her arms and hugged her tightly.

The instructor was now out of the car. 'If the lesson is cancelled, I still have to be paid.'

'How would you like me to cancel the rest of your baldy little fuckin' life?' Agnes spat at him.

He retreated to the office. Marion and Agnes stood embracing by the car. The evening traffic rumbled past them on Talbot Street. Without being aware of it, as she held Marion, Agnes had mascara running down her face, and was patting Marion's back and hoarsely whispering, 'There, there, there . . .'

Chapter 17

AGNES'S WORDS WERE COMING IN SOBS.

Marion's death had come swiftly. Everyone had been prepared for a drawn-out painful death from the cancer that was eating away at her, but, true to form, Marion's heart attack caught them all by surprise. It was now three days since Marion's funeral. Agnes's shoulders heaved with shudders of grief, as she sat in the snug of Foley's lounge.

'I was plannin' on gettin' her to Lourdes,' she said to Monica Foley, wife of the publican and the only other person on the premises, for it was one in the morning and the drinkers had long since gone. Monica simply nodded her head and replied, 'I know, I know . . . terrible.'

'I . . . I was hopin' for a miracle . . . yeh, a miracle . . . Yeh know what I mean, Monica?'

'I do . . . I do, Agnes. Well, maybe you got your miracle?' Monica tried, by way of consolation. 'Marion went quickly and peacefully, and when it comes down to it, wouldn't we all want that?' She was genuinely sad for Agnes, but it was late and she really wanted Agnes out of the pub and home.

'I never thought of that. Yeh . . . I know what yeh mean there, Monica . . . a miracle . . . yeh . . . could be!' Agnes took a slug of her cider. Monica glanced at the glass, only one slug left, thank God. Agnes moved closer to Monica. Her voice now took on a conspiratorial tone.

'Monica . . . if I tell you something . . .

now, it's weird . . . but promise me yeh won't tell a soul . . . will ya?'

'Is it a long story, Agnes? 'Cause it's very late.'

'This won't take long, Monica, but it's . . . well yeh know, it's . . . just promise me!'

'I promise . . . I do, I promise.'

'Good . . . well, I'll tell yeh,' Agnes picked up the glass to take the last drop, then changed her mind, put the glass down and to Monica's disappointment took out her cigarettes and matches. Thirty seconds later Agnes was puffing, and ready to begin her tale.

'Right! Well, Monica, fifteen years ago . . .'

'Fifteen years? . . . Ah, Agnes, this is goin' to be a long one.'

'Shush, shush . . . it's not . . . and anyway it's worth it! I swear.'

'Well, go on then, I'm listenin'.'

'Okay, so where was I? Oh yeh. For the last fifteen years I have been meeting Marion Monks every mornin'. We'd push our prams down through The Jarro. Sometimes we'd chat, sometimes we'd have nothin' to say, so we'd . . . we'd eh . . . say . . .' Agnes stopped.

191

'Nothin?' Monica offered.

'Exactly!' Agnes said and belched. 'Anyway,' she went on, 'one thing never changed . . . when we got to St Jarlath's church, Marion would run up the steps, pull open the door . . .' Agnes paused, the memory filling her eyes and her throat closing slightly, 'and she'd yell . . .' again a pause, this time quickly filled by Monica: 'Hello, God, it's me, Marion.'

'Yeh . . . that's it! How'd you know?' Agnes asked.

'Everybody in The Jarro knew about that, Agnes. Is that the story? 'Cause if it is I heard it before.'

Monica stood up to give Agnes the hint. Agnes patted the seat where Monica had been sitting.

'Sit down! . . . Sit down . . . you haven't heard this bit . . . sit, sit down!'

Monica sat with a sigh. 'Agnes, really, it's late. Please hurry it up.'

'I will . . . I will . . . Anyway, I've watched her doin' this day after day and year after year. I thought it was stupid! . . . And I told her that . . . but still, every mornin' she'd be up them steps: "Hello God, it's me, Marion!" ' There was a pause. Agnes at last drank the end of her drink and squashed the cigarette-end into the ashtray. 'I could hear those words in me head as I walked up them steps three days ago . . . behind Marion's coffin. How could you do this, God? I thought. This woman never forgot you. What does she get for it? Then as we walked through the doors of the church, and started down the aisle . . . I got me answer! The organ struck a very low tone and in the middle of the drone I heard, as clear as day, a warm, strong voice say: "Hello, Marion, it's me, God," and I just *knew* she was going to be all right!'

Agnes lifted her head to Monica who was sitting open-mouthed, not with shock, but asleep. Agnes chortled. She leaned over and gently touched Monica's arm.

'Monica, love . . .'

Monica jumped. 'What? What! Oh Agnes, what was that? . . . I missed the end of it . . . what was it?'

'Ah nothing, Monica, I was just shite-talkin', listen, let me out, love, will yeh, and go on t'your bed.'

Agnes gathered her cigarettes and her handbag and put her coat on. Monica walked her to the side door, opened it, peered out first to make sure there were no police about, and quietly said goodnight to Agnes. When she stepped out into the night air Agnes took a deep breath. The door closed gently behind her, but when the bolt was pushed into place it banged like a gunshot!

'Holy Jaysus — Monica!' Agnes yelped, the words coming in bursts of steam from her mouth into the cold night air. Behind the door she heard Monica say, 'Shh!'

'Ah shush, me arse, yeh frightened the fuckin' life outa me,' Agnes replied gruffly and gathering herself together she started for home.

It wasn't as easy a journey as it usually was. The path had become somewhat un-even, causing Agnes to walk a zig-zag route. Another thing, the steps she was taking were a little unsteady. And the kerbs? Well, they

were ridiculously high. Still, Agnes, sol-
diered on. After about one hundred yards or
so she began to feel ill. Must be something I
ate, she thought, even though she had not
eaten a real meal for days, just a couple of
sandwiches here and there. She stopped and
leaned against a building. Her stomach
heaved and she knew it was coming up. She
prepared for it, taking out the palate that
held her two front teeth. She bent over and
threw up with enthusiasm.

'Are you all right, beeautiful Agnes
Browne?' a voice from behind asked, as a
gentle hand was placed on her shoulder.
The accent was clearly French. Agnes knew
it was the Pierre fella from the pizza place.
Where's me fuckin' teeth? she thought. They
had been in her hand just seconds ago. She
opened her hand and looked, but all it now
contained was a tissue she had taken from
her coat pocket. She must have put them in
her pocket while taking out the tissue. She
didn't turn. She didn't move.

'Mademoiselle Agnes, with ze sparkle
eyes! Are you okay?'

Agnes was afraid to answer, for with the two teeth missing 'Yes' would have sounded like a sow breaking wind, so she grunted, 'Neh,' and nodded her head slowly. She put her hand into her pocket, and felt the teeth. She tried to drop the tissue and pick up the teeth in one gentle movement. She couldn't. The teeth were now caught in the tissue.

'Turn around! Let me gaze at you.' He started to pull at her shoulder. Oh no! Agnes thought, without me two front teeth I look like a fuckin' vampire! He had started to turn her. She swiftly pulled the teeth from her pocket and pretended to cough, while ramming the palate into her mouth. He turned her fully around. She tried to speak. She couldn't. The tissue was sticking out of her mouth. She said: 'I'm grand, thank you,' but it came out as 'Arf arf arf arf,' and she turned and went to walk away. He ran in front of her.

'I am fery new to Dooblin, would you show me around sometime?' he asked.

'I'm sorry no, love,' she replied.

All he heard was: 'Arf arf arf!'

'Oh marvelloose, what about next weekend? Friday?'

'Arf arf arf!'

'Good. We meet in Foley's at eight o'clock?'

'Arf arf arf!' Agnes was red with frustration.

'*Au revoir*, then,' and off he walked. Agnes was trying to roar after him that it was *not* a date! She stood shouting after him 'Arf arf arf arf!!' Two men walked past her, and one shouted, 'Sit, Fido, sit!' and they both laughed.

Whether she liked it or not, Agnes Browne had a date for Friday night!

Chapter 18

ALTHOUGH THE WINTER WAS HERE, the Saturday-morning sun was still a little warm and welcoming as Mark pushed his cart out of the flat and headed through The Jarro. He had sent Dermot to Granny's with Trevor and herded all the other children out of the flat so his Mother could have a 'sleep in'. She needed it. She had come home drunk last night. He woke when he heard the front door open. She pottered around the flat muttering to herself. Mark got up to see that she was all right. He expected to find her in the kitchen, but she wasn't there, though the kettle was on the lighted stove. The bathroom door was half-open so he peeped in. His mother was bent over the sink with her false teeth in her hand. She was picking pieces of tissue off them and muttering things like: 'Cheeky French bastard', the last word sending a spray of spittle onto the mirror. He quietly slipped back into bed.

Mark was very proud of his cart. He had made it himself. The body was a strong wooden box that he'd picked up on the docks. Three lengths of two-by-two made up the handles and axle. It took about five hours of walking up and down the railway line to find two matching bearings for the wheels, but it was worth it. It was acknowledged by one and all that Mark Browne's cart was the finest in The Jarro. Each Saturday morning Mark would push the cart down to the 'turf depot' in Sean McDermott

Street. Since Redser's death Agnes Browne was allowed two bags of turf per week, as part of her widows' and orphans' pension. This was a nice bonus, as the turf burnt well, and the two bags, along with a bag of coal and a half bag of slack would last the whole week. The catch was, you had to collect the turf from the depot, supplying your own sacks and cart. Mark was first in the queue every Saturday morning, arriving there half an hour before it opened. He would bring a football with him and play up against the depot wall until the 'turf man' arrived at half-past eight.

Mark did most of his thinking while tapping that ball against the wall. This morning his thoughts were about his future. It was nearing the end of October now, over eight weeks since his friends had gone back to school after the summer break. Mark had decided not to return but to go to work. But he had spent the time just looking, and not finding a job. The problem was his mother's insistence on taking up a trade.

'I don't want you going from job to job

and back to the dole like your father!' she preached. 'You'll get a trade like your Uncle Gonzo.'

Uncle Gonzo's name was actually Bismarck. The name had been picked by his father to rile the baptising priest, whom Uncle Gonzo's father believed to have been a British spy in 1916. The gesture was met with hurrahs in the local pub, but Uncle Gonzo had to carry the can for his father's heroism. Fortunately for him he was born with a bright red nose which grew larger and redder as he fed it with Irish whiskey. Bismarck soon became Gonzo, after the popular vaudeville clown with the big red nose, though his was plastic. Uncle Gonzo was a plumber. He was a very good plumber. He was so successful that he became the first of the Browne family to buy his own home. Agnes Browne was very proud of Uncle Gonzo and it was clear to her that the road to success began with a signpost that said: Get a trade.

Mark didn't want to be a plumber. He continued to tap the ball up against the wall and consider his future. He was so engrossed that he didn't see the elderly man coming across the road from one of the four large town houses that faced the turf depot. The man watched Mark for a few moments then spoke to him: 'Little boy?'

Mark, startled, took his eye off the ball. It came off the wall and past him. Mark ran after the ball and retrieved it. Slowly and reluctantly he walked back to the man. He looked at him suspiciously. It didn't help that the man had a peculiar accent that made him sound like the villain in a Boris Karloff movie.

The man gestured to the boy to come towards him. 'Come here . . . quickly.'

'What d'yeh want, Mister?'

'Come closer, boy. You want that I should shout instead of talk?'

Mark walked towards him, and gaped at this strange-speaking man. He was, Mark guessed, about a hundred years old. His hair was grey and bushy, with a bald track down the centre. His back was bent slightly. His face was tanned and looked as if it could be a kind face. He had grey eyes behind little circular glasses, which were perched on a huge nose, shaped like a crow's beak. He wore a striped shirt, but without its collar attached, over which he wore no less than three cardigans. To Mark's young eyes, this was a strange creature indeed. When the man spoke his voice was gentle.

'Every Saturday I see you here — always the same time, eight o'clock,' the man stated.

'Yeh, so what?'

'Never a Saturday do you miss. Rain or shine, you are here, always the same.'

'Yeh already said that. So what?'

'This tells me you are a reliable boy. Are you? Are you a reliable boy?'

'No, I'm a Browne.'

The little old man chuckled, and as he did he tapped his thigh lightly.

'How would you like to earn two shillings, young Browne?'

'Two bob?'

'Yes, two bob.'

'For what? What do I have to do?'

'What you have to do is come into my home and light my fire for me.'

'Light your fire?'

'Yes.'

'Two bob — to light your fire?'

'That's it!' The man nodded and clasped his hands together as he said this.

'Why?'

'Why? Why what?'

'Why would you give me two bob to light your fire?'

The little man walked to Mark's cart and sat on the edge of it. He had not anticipated being questioned. He assumed that two shillings would be taken, 'no questions asked'. With a crooked finger he pushed his glasses up his nose.

'I am Jewish and today is my Sabbath.'

'You're a Jewman? From the pawn shop?'

Again the man chuckled. 'I do not own the pawn shop, although I believe the man that does is indeed Jewish and that's how you say it, *Jewish*, not "Jewman"!'

'And what's a Sabbich?'

'A . . . eh . . . a holy day. Saturday is to me

what Sunday is to you.' The man gesticulated with his hands while he spoke. They moved gracefully. They reminded Mark of a magician.

'What has that got to do with your fire?'

'Well, in my religion we cannot do certain things on a Saturday. Lighting a fire is one of them.'

'Then how are you supposed to keep warm?'

'My faith in God keeps me warm.'

'Yeh, but it won't light your fire, Mister.'

This time the man laughed. It was a bright laugh, and as Mark would describe later, 'All of him laughed', his eyes, his chin, his eyebrows, and he opened his arms wide as he laughed.

'Perhaps you are right, young Browne. But tell me, will two shillings light my fire?'

'Flippin' right it will!' Mark smiled at the man for the first time. He dropped the ball into the cart and the two walked to the house. As they strolled across the road the elderly man put his hand on Mark's shoulder.

'So let's introduce ourselves properly; you

can call me Mr Wise.'

'Why, what's wrong with your real name?' Mark asked.

'That *is* my name — Henry Wise; and what goes along with Browne?'

'Mark.'

'My word! Look at this! I get a prophet!'

'At two shillings for lighting your fire, so do I.'

Mr Wise laughed heartily and ushered Mark into the house. Mark was gobsmacked by the interior. Every inch was carpeted. There was lace on the table, pictures on the walls. In the room where the fireplace was there was a piano, and a china cabinet full of gleaming and sparkling things. But the thing that caught Mark's eye most pleasingly was sitting in the corner all alone. It was a television set!

'Wow!' Mark exclaimed, running his hand over the walnut cabinet that held the magic tube.

'What?' Mr. Wise enquired.

'A television! I've never seen one up close, only in Foley's pub. Can I turn it on?'

'No, not today. Sabbath.'

'Oh yeh, I forgot. Right, where's the coal hole?'

Within minutes Mark had a fire blazing in the hearth, the coal bucket full, and the ashes put in the bin outside. Mr Wise arrived into the room carrying a tray with a glass of orange squash and a solitary biscuit on it.

'Ah beautiful, Mark. A good fire! Well done. Here, this is for you.' Mr Wise proffered the tray. Mark looked at the orange and biscuit. He made to take them, but stopped and looked at Mr Wise suspiciously.

'I still get me two bob as well?' Mark wanted everything to be quite clear.

Mr Wise smiled. 'With all of my thanks you do indeed.' Mark smiled, and took the goodies. He devoured the biscuit and orange, wiped his mouth with his sleeve and put his hand out. Mr Wise placed the coin in Mark's palm.

'Thanks, Mr Wise.'

'No, it is I that thank you, Mark Browne. Same time next week?'

'Yeh sure. See yeh next week, Mr Wise.'

Mark closed the front door behind him

and trotted across the road. A queue had formed behind his cart. Even though Mark was not with the cart, the others knew whose cart it was — the boy who was always first on the queue. Mark loaded up with turf and on this Saturday morning brought his mother home two sacks of turf *and* two shillings.

After carrying the turf up to his landing and then the cart, Mark went into the flat. He found Agnes looking drawn, sitting at the kitchen table nursing a cup of tea. He marched over and placed the two-shilling piece on the table in front of her.

'What's that for?' Agnes asked.

'For you. I earned it,' Mark beamed.

'Earned it? How?'

'I lit a fire for a Jewman. He couldn't do it 'cause it's a "savage day," so he paid me to do it for him.'

'What are you talkin' about?' Agnes was confused, her head not entirely in one piece. Mark related his morning's adventure to her in detail, finishing with 'and now he wants me to do it every Saturday.'

Agnes mulled all this over in her mind. She was bothered that Mark might mistake this for a job.

'Lighting fires is not a trade, Mark.'

'I know that, Ma, but it's good isn't it?' Agnes looked at the boy. With his milk round and paper round, and now his lighting fires on a Saturday the boy was handing up a pound a week. He was so willing, and so hard-working. She was proud, but worried about his future. There's a time to worry and a time to be proud, she thought. This was a time to be proud.

'It's better than good, love, it's great,' she smiled.

The boy was thrilled. He went to the sink and took a cup from the draining board.

'Ah, sure,' he spoke like an adult, 'I'll have a cup of tea with yeh.'

Agnes poured his tea and he sat down. 'You don't look the best, Ma. Is it the drink?' Mark asked.

'Kind of . . . I . . . wasn't well last night, love.'

'I know, I heard yeh,' he said quietly.

'I'll be all right . . . It's just . . . I miss

Marion, love, but I'll be grand, you'll see, I will. Drink makes you do stupid things.'

'Yeh! Like gettin' sick!' Mark stated.

'Oh worse than that, love. Like makin' dates with Frenchmen!'

'*What*, Ma?'

'Nothing . . . it doesn't matter . . . have we any painkillers?'

Chapter 19

THE LAST 'DATE' AGNES BROWNE had been on was when Redser had taken her to the dog-racing in Shelbourne Park. It had cost her a fortune. As soon as Redser lost all his money — and that took only four races — he began to 'borrow' hers. By the night's end they were both penniless, and had to walk home. That was the night Redser proposed — well 'proposed' is a bit strong! What had happened was they were walking along the canal towards Pearse Street, but not *into* Pearse Street — Redser couldn't go near Pearse Street as he was a marked man following an incident involving some 'Teds' from there and a cut-throat razor — so that night they had turned off the canal and walked down by the Meath Hospital. As they strolled past the back of the biscuit factory, Agnes felt the moment was right.

'Redser?'

'What?'

'D'yeh love me?'

'Don't be stupid, a'course I do!'

Agnes took a deep breath. 'Well, I'm pregnant.'

She waited for a reaction.

He didn't look at her, he didn't stop walking, he simply said, 'Are yeh?'

'Yeh,' Agnes answered softly.

There was silence for the next fifty yards. Then he said, 'We better get married so.'

Agnes was thrilled. She stopped, glowing inside. 'Will we? Really, Redser?'

'Yeh, I said so, didn't I?'

Agnes threw her arms around him. 'Oh, Redser!'

'Hey will yeh fuck off — give over.' Redser was embarrassed by any overt affection unless there was a lot of drink taken. 'I'll get

yeh a ring at the weekend,' he said. Redser
knew a man who had access to these things.

'I don't want a ring,' Agnes said.

'Why not?'

'It's a waste of money. Yeh can't do anything with a ring. I want a bike!'

'A fuckin' bike?'

'Yeh, a bike, but a good wan!'

'An engagement bike!' Redser was con-
founded.

Agnes knew what she was doing. Firstly,
with a bike she could have a bit of independence, and secondly, she knew that any engagement ring from Redser would eventually end up in the pawn. She lost on both
counts, for when they were only two weeks
married Redser sold the bike anyway to get
money for the bookies.

But the point is, Redser never asked her out
again. He 'took' her out, but every girl knows
that there's a huge difference between being
'asked out' and being 'took out'.

And so with Friday looming, Agnes felt
like a teenager going on a first date. One
minute she was going, next she wasn't. She

told the children about her date with the Frenchman. There was some resistance.

'Yeh can't, Ma. Mammies don't go on dates,' Mark protested. He was not happy at all. Not at all.

'Well, this Mammy is!'

'I think it's great, Ma!' Cathy chirped.

'Thanks, love.'

'Frenchmen lick your teeth when they're kissin', Cathy Dowdall says,' Cathy added.

'Stop that talk! That Cathy Dowdall has too much to say for herself,' Agnes snapped.

Agnes intended to use her little breaks from the stall each day to scour the shops around Moore Street for something suitable to wear for the date. It was hard to decide. Nothing too fancy, not for Foley's anyway. Nothing too skimpy, she didn't want to give the Frenchman the wrong idea. Then again she didn't want to look like a housewife. It was so hard to decide. On top of this, it was the week before Halloween. It was a busy time and the fruit and nuts were flying off the stall. Along with the fruit, Agnes would shift a few fireworks. These were illegal, but she would sell them under the counter — or from under the skirt to be exact. In case of a policeman stopping and searching a dealer, the dealers would keep the boxes of 'bangers' in their knickers. Agnes still laughs at Marion's comments — once when she had her knickers full of fireworks she said that if she sat on a cigarette end by accident, 'They'd find me fanny in America!'

So, what with the fruit sales and fireworks, Agnes got precious little time to look. She eventually settled on a navy midi skirt with a cream twin-set. She left her good coat into Marlowe's Cleaners, so in essence she was all set.

Agnes began getting ready at six o'clock on the Friday. She was hoping for a relaxing bath, but it wasn't to be. No sooner had she filled the bath and got it foaming, thanks to the Quix washing up liquid she added, and immersed herself, than Trevor came into the bathroom and began to strip. Within minutes, Cathy too was in the bath. 'No rest for the wicked,' Agnes said aloud as she washed Cathy's hair.

By half-past-seven she was dressed and putting the finishing touches to her make-up. In the sitting room the children were waiting for Agnes to make her grand entrance from the bedroom. There was an air of excitement about, although Mark showed no signs of interest whatsoever. When Agnes emerged she sailed into the centre of the room and did a twirl, saying, 'Well, what do yis think?'

The children were dumbstruck. Cathy said 'Wow!' and began to clap, and the others joined in. Mark couldn't believe his eyes. Was this beautiful woman really his mother? Agnes looked stunning! He stood up and walked towards her, his eyes wide.

Agnes stood straight and awaited his rebuke. 'And you, Mark, what do *you* think?'

The boy smiled. 'I think Dublin has a very lucky Frenchman tonight. You're beautiful, Ma, really, just beautiful.'

'Thanks, love.' Agnes hugged him in relief.

The other children jumped up and they all hugged each other, cheering loudly!

'Mind me frock, for Christ's sake,' Agnes

yelled. They went to the door to see her off. She walked to the top of the stairs and turned back to them. Six glowing faces, with smiles as wide as the doorway. She was as proud of them as they of her.

'Straight to bed with yis, and I'll see yis in the morning,' she ordered.

They all nodded with a chorus of 'Okay, Mammy!' and Agnes turned to descend the stairs.

Mark called after her: 'Mammy!'

Agnes turned. 'Yes love?'

'Don't take any liquorice off him!'

'What? I don't like liquorice.'

'Good!!' Mark smiled and closed the door.

Agnes turned a few heads when she made her way through the lounge in Foley's to the snug. PJ brought her over her glass of cider. 'I take it you're not going to the Bingo tonight then, Agnes?'

'No PJ, not tonight.' Agnes gave little away.

PJ didn't enquire any further. Agnes hoped that the French fella would slip in quietly and they could leave with as little fuss as possible. She could see the entrance from where she sat. She decided that as soon as he walked in she would wave at him. Bang on the rendezvous time the door opened and in walked Pierre. His dark hair was slicked back with Brylcreem. He wore a tan polo-neck under a dark brown jacket and cream pants. He stuck out like a sore thumb. He was carrying a huge bunch of flowers. He glanced around the lounge.

'Sweet Mother of Jaysus!' Agnes said aloud when she saw him. 'He thinks he's fuckin' Elvis!' If only Marion was here now for moral support! She slid down in her seat hoping he wouldn't see her, and that he might leave, thinking she hadn't shown up. He didn't see her. His face changed to a disappointed expression and he turned to leave. From behind the bar PJ called to him, 'Hey, Sham!! She's in the snug!'

'Snook?' Pierre held a hand to his ear.

'No, the snug, back there.' PJ gestured with his thumb.

Pierre made his way to the snug. He stood

at the doorway, transfixed. '*Sacre bleu!* Agnes Browne, you are a veesion of heaven!' he said aloud.

There was a cheer and a round of applause from the lounge.

'What'd he say?' asked a deaf old man.

'SHE'S A VISION OF HEAVEN!' his wife roared in his ear.

Pierre wasn't finished. 'I would cross the h'Alps bare feeted, I would suffer torture, any pain to be with such a beeauty as you.' He proffered the flowers.

'What'd he say?' Again the shout from the deaf old man.

'HE'S FUCKIN' MAD INTO HER!' his wife shouted back. This was received by another cheer and applause.

In a panic reaction, Agnes jumped up and walked towards him. 'Come on you, yeh fuckin' eejit, let's go.'

They left to applause and cheers, Pierre giving salutes to all and sundry, Agnes as red as a beetroot.

It turned out to be the most magnificent evening Agnes had ever known. They went to a posh French restaurant, with tablecloths and candles on the tables. When they got out of the taxi, Pierre held the door open for her. Each time she came back from the toilet, Pierre stood and held her chair. Agnes didn't eat much, half because of her excitement, half because she didn't like eating anything she couldn't pronounce. There was soft music and Pierre bought a bottle of champagne. Agnes wasn't sure she'd like it, and was pleasantly surprised when she found it tasted quite like cider! There was a tiny dance floor in the restaurant and Pierre took Agnes up and they danced cheek to cheek. Agnes was thrilled — but wished that Pierre was Cliff Richard. Well, you can't have everything. They left the restaurant, got a taxi to St Jarlath's church, and began to walk home from there. Pierre slipped his hand into hers. He looked up at the clear winter sky.

'I love the stars,' he said.

'Me too.' Agnes answered. 'Spencer Tracey, Olivia de Haviland . . .'

'No, no I mean the real stars.'

'What d'yeh mean real stars? Spencer

Tracy? He's brilliant.'

'No, these stars . . . in the sky.' He pointed.

'Oh, yeh eejit, *them!*'

Before long they reached James Larkin Court, and the two stood at the bottom of the steps. Agnes let go of his hand.

'Well, Pierre, that was the best night I've ever had.'

'Me too. It was *fantastique!*'

'Thanks.'

'No, no, sank *you.*'

'Ah no, thank *you!*'

Then they were both silent. He smiled at her and put his hands in his pockets.

'Well then . . .' he said.

'Yeh, well then . . . listen, good night!'

Agnes turned to climb the steps.

Pierre called after her. 'Agnes!'

When she turned back to him, he had his arms stretched out.

'What?' she asked.

'No keess goodnight to feenish such a beeautiful evening?'

Slowly Agnes descended the steps. Her legs felt unsteady, and her heart was thumping. When she stood face-to-face with Pierre he wrapped his arms around her and gently touched his lips upon hers. Her lips relaxed. His mouth felt warm and strong. Her eyelids fluttered and slowly closed. She was just about to melt into his arms when suddenly she felt something dart into her mouth. It was Pierre's tongue. Her eyes opened quickly. He's lickin' me fuckin' teeth! she thought. She let out a yelp and pushed away.

'Ahh! Yeh dirty bastard!'

'What? What is it? What did I do?' He was shocked. Agnes's slap had caught him by surprise and stung his cheek.

'Yeh . . . yeh pervert!' Agnes took the steps two by two and slammed the door, leaving behind one very sore and confused Frenchman.

Chapter 20

IT HAD SNOWED OVERNIGHT, and the cart was difficult to push. It was empty now. What would it be like coming back from the depot, full of turf? Mark decided he would cross that bridge when he came to it. He parked the cart and shuffled across the icy road to Mr Wise's house. He didn't have to knock, he never did. Mr Wise would open the door just as Mark got to it.

'Good morning, Mark,' Mr Wise greeted him. Mark noticed that today Mr Wise was wearing at least five cardigans. Where does he get them? he thought.

'Good mornin', Mr Wise. Cold today!'

'Yes it is! Get it going quickly and I will make us both a cup of hot chocolate.'

Mark's eyes brightened. 'Yeh, lovely.'

When the fire was blazing and the chill gone off the room, Mark sat in a chair by the window so as to keep an eye on his cart. Mr Wise arrived in with two mugs of hot chocolate and the usual single biscuit — Mark reckoned it would be next Easter before he'd used up an entire packet.

He took the mug gratefully, and cupping his hands around it he took a sip. It was piping hot.

'Have you any kids, Mr Wise?' Mark asked.

'Just one, my boy Manny. Well, he's not a boy really, he's . . . oh, he must be forty now. He lives in England. He comes home maybe once, maybe twice a year. He's a busy boy.'

'Is he coming home for Christmas, Mr Wise?'

'No.'

'Is that why you've no decorations or Christmas tree?'

'Oh no. That's because I am Jewish.'

'What's that got to do with it?'

'Well, you see, we don't believe in Christmas.'

Mark laughed heartily and was sure the old man was kidding. 'Will yeh go on outta that! How can yeh not believe in something when it's real?'

Mr Wise smiled, amused at the simple innocence of the boy. 'It's a long story, too long for me to tell, so let's not go into it, Mark.'

'Okay, Mr Wise.'

'What about you, Mark. Are you ready for Christmas?'

'Nearly. I got soldiers for Trevor, a doll for

Cathy. I'm gettin' a parachuter for Rory. I'll get colouring books for Simon and Dermot, they're twins and yeh have to get them the same, and I'm givin' Frankie a Selection Box. I don't know what to get me Mammy, though.'

'Why not some perfume?'

'Nah, I got her aftershave last year and she never uses it. No, I want to get her something different. I have to think!'

'Yes, well, I'm sure you'll think of something. How is she?'

'Grand! She's givin' me a hard time about not gettin' a job, but she's grand. It looks like I'll be goin' back to school.'

'You sound disappointed! School will be good for you.'

'Not for me, Mr Wise, I'm no good at it — brutal. Some of the lads in me class were good at it, but I'm not, I'm poxy! No, I want to work!'

'What about training as a carpenter?'

'What about it?'

'Would you like to do that? Make shelves, and furniture?'

'Yeh, I would, but is it a trade?'

'Oh yes, one of the finest of the trades.'

'I built me cart meself, yeh know.' Mark pointed out the window.

'And a good cart it is too,' Mr Wise complimented.

'Best in The Jarro,' Mark said proudly.

Mr Wise looked at the boy. His own boy, Manny, was a schmuck, spoiled by his mother. Manny never came home, not since his mother had passed away. He wondered if Mark had been given the education and attention that Manny had got, what could hold him back?

'Mark, I will give you a job,' he said.

Mark spun from the window. 'Will yeh, Mr Wise? Will yeh?'

'Yes, Mark, I will.'

'Doin' what?'

'Apprentice carpenter in my factory.'

Mark jumped from the chair and hugged the old man, a man that had not been genuinely hugged for forty years. 'Thank you, Mr Wise, thank you.'

'Hold it, hold it. This will be a real job — and there *is* a catch.'

Mark's face dropped. 'What's the catch?' he asked sullenly.

'If you train with me you must also go to school, for two half-days a week.'

'Ah no!!'

'Wait! It's a carpentry school. Not like the school you have in mind. In this school they teach you to be a carpenter. What do you say?'

The boy smiled again. 'I say I'm your bleedin' man, Mr Wise.'

'Okay. You start Monday. Be here at eight o'clock sharp. Your wages will be one pound and fifteen shillings a week.'

Mark floated across the road to the turf depot. What should have been a difficult journey home was made easy by the excitement of getting a job. The snow melted beneath his feet and the cart felt like it was full of cotton wool. He couldn't wait to tell his Mammy!

It was by accident on that Saturday morning that Agnes found out about the concert. She had done her usual rummage around the Hill market, then headed down Henry

Street to do a bit of shoppin' for the Christmas. She bought the seven sets of underwear and socks. She bought the guns and holsters for Simon, Dermot and Frankie; Rory had asked for an embroidery set in his letter to Santy, but she hadn't decided on that yet. The shopping had taken it out of her a bit, so she decided to treat herself to a coffee and cake in Arnott's. As she sat at her table nursing her coffee, surrounded by bags, Agnes couldn't help overhearing the two women at the table beside her. They were southsiders and talked posh.

'I don't know why we shop on this side, Deirdre, it's so difficult to get the shops over here to deliver.'

'Oh come now, Philomena, it's fun. All the dealers calling out and the hustle and bustle — come on!'

'I suppose.' There was a lull in the conversation, and Agnes stopped listening and returned to her own thoughts. Buddha promised he'd get her the tricycle for Trevor, so that should be all right. Mark was a different kettle of fish. What to get him was a problem. After the disaster with the tent she had to be careful. He had made her suffer for that. Then she heard it:

'Harry got me tickets for the concert as a surprise.'

'What concert?'

'In the Capitol. Cliff Richard is coming there Christmas week!'

Agnes knocked over her coffee cup as she jumped up and gathered her bags. She ran out of Arnott's into Henry Street like a shoplifter. She scurried down the GPO Arcade and was at the Capitol within five minutes of hearing the woman's statement. She went to the box office, breathless.

' 'Scuse me, love, what date is the Friday of Christmas week?' she asked.

The girl in the box office looked at a calendar overhead. 'Eh . . . it's eh . . . the twenty-second.'

'Right! Give me one ticket for the twenty-second for the Cliff Richard concert — up at the front.'

'We're sold out.'

'Well, the twenty-first then.'

'I said we're sold out. All sold out, for the whole week — Monday to Saturday!'

'Yeh can't be! Check — any night — I only want the one ticket!'

'Look, love, we're *sold out,* right? Jaysus, they've been on sale for two weeks, we sold out days ago.'

'But you don't understand. I'm his best fan in Ireland.'

'You and fifty thousand others, love. Sold out, now go on or I'll call the usher!'

Agnes staggered out onto O'Connell Street. She headed for home in a stupor. People walking towards her must have thought she was demented. She moped along, dragging her bags behind her. She couldn't believe it was possible for Cliff Richard to be in Dublin singing to strangers and not to *her* — Agnes Browne, his number one fan in the world.

When she entered the flat, she just dropped the bags and slumped into her armchair. Mark came bounding out of the kitchen. 'Hiya, Ma! Have I got news for yeh!'

'Put some turf on that fire,' Agnes said in

a daze.

Mark went to the turf bucket and put a couple of sods on the blazing fire. Dusting his hands, he walked over and knelt in front of her. 'Well, do you want to hear it?' he asked excitedly.

'Yeh, go on then, tell us,' she said flatly.

'I got a job!' Mark beamed.

Without taking her eyes off the flickering flames in the grate, Agnes patted the boy on the head and said calmly, 'That's nice, son, that's nice.'

'*Nice?* It's fuckin' great, Ma! It's a trade job as well . . . I'm goin' to be a carpenter!'

Agnes suddenly snapped out of her trance. 'A carpenter! Good boy! How?'

Mark told the story with enthusiasm. Agnes was really pleased, especially about the schooling. She hugged the boy and made a cup of tea for them both. She then told Mark about her disappointment over the tickets for Cliff Richard. He was sad for her but perked up when she said, 'But, son, your good news makes up for any disappointment, it really does.'

It didn't. Life had snipped yet another of the strings that held up the heart of this woman.

Chapter 21

AGNES WAS PLEASED TO MEET the famous Mr Wise at last. He was a nice man, a kind man, and Agnes could see why Mark thought the world of him. Mark had been working for over two weeks in Mr Wise's factory. He loved it. He had made a shelf in that two-week period and Mr Wise had allowed him to keep it as a souvenir of his first effort as a 'tradesman'. It hung beside the cooker and held the tea caddy. The reason Agnes had called to see Mr Wise was to thank him for his kindness to Mark and to ask his advice. She had finally decided what to get Mark for Christmas, a set of carpenter's tools, good ones. She knew nothing about tools and figured Mr Wise was the best man for advice on the matter. He gladly told her what basic tools Mark should have and over a cup of tea went through the things to look out for when buying them. He told her to go to Lenehans of Capel Street.

She went there next morning and spent at least an hour picking them out. The shop assistant was very helpful, advising and telling her all the pluses and minuses. When the tools were selected, he parcelled them up for her. She had intended taking them with her until she got the bill. It totalled fifteen pounds and twelve shillings. He asked for 'fifteen and ten', giving her a little discount.

'I don't have enough with me,' she said.

'That's no problem. If you give me a deposit I can put them away for you,' he smiled.

Agnes fished in her purse. She took out a ten-shilling note.

'Would ten bob be all right for a deposit?'

'Absolutely, love.' He took the note and wrote out a receipt, then he wrote 'Browne' on the parcel, and went out back to store it.

Agnes left the shop a bit worried. Fifteen pounds was a lot to find between now and Christmas Eve — eight days. But she'd find it, somehow she'd find it. She checked the Herald clock in Abbey Street. Time to go up to Buddha and collect the tricycle for

Trevor. As she turned into O'Connell Street she saw four men out on top of the Capitol theatre porch erecting a giant sign with Cliff's picture on it. A white band across the sign with red letters on it read 'Sold out'.

She put her head down and walked past. Her mind turned back to money matters. She had three pounds in her slipper at home. The following week was Christmas week but it was never a busy one for her stall, all that sold were potatoes and sprouts. So she couldn't count on more than three pound ten off that. Mark was handing up a pound, that was seven pounds ten shillings. She had made the last payment on her hamper the previous week, so that was all the Christmas food paid for. Buddha owed her seven pounds and ten shillings, the tricycle was two pounds, that meant he had to give her five pound ten. That was thirteen pounds. She could really do with another ten pounds to get her over Christmas, buy the tools and see her into the New Year. She looked to heaven and smiling said aloud, 'Marion, lend us a tenner, will ya?' Heaven was the right place to look, she thought to herself, for she could do with a minor miracle.

When she arrived back at the flat, she had the tricycle with her. Yellow and red, it would make Trevor's eyes glow with joy when he woke to find it waiting under the tree on Christmas morning. The trick was to make sure that neither Trevor nor the other children found it until then. Agnes tiptoed up the stairs. When she arrived at her landing she opened the door to the water tank for the toilet in the flat below hers. Gently she slid the bike in beside the tank. Mark stored his turf sacks on the other side. She lifted one of the sacks and used it to cover the bike. She closed the door quietly and went up to her own flat.

There was great excitement when she came in. Charlie Bennett, the coalman, had delivered the Christmas tree, and the kids were waiting to decorate it. Agnes calmed them all down and promised them they would all do it, but after tea. Tea first, tree later, she pronounced. Agnes made the tea and they were all sitting around the kitchen table when Mark tapped his fork off his cup, like he had seen a best man do at a wedding. Everybody stopped talking and looked at him.

'What's that for?' Agnes asked.

'I'm goin' to make a speech, Ma!' he answered.

'Oh, I see. Quiet, youse, listen to your brother — the man of the house.'

Mark puffed out his chest. 'Ahem! I have a surprise for everyone!' he began.

'The hairs are after fallin' off your willy!' Dermot said and all the children laughed. Agnes gave Dermot a clip on the ear, but gave a little laugh herself as well.

'Don't mind him, son, you go on, you have a surprise for us all? What is it?'

'Today I put a five-shilling deposit on a television set,' Mark announced proudly.

The cheers and whoops could be heard in Cork! Cathy took Trevor's hands and danced in a circle, singing, 'We're gettin' a tell-ee! We're gettin' a tell-ee!'

Agnes shushed everybody. 'You *what?*' she asked Mark.

'I put a deposit on a telly,' Mark repeated.

'How much is this . . . telly . . . going to cost?'

'Fifteen shillings a month. It has a slot at the back and you put two bob in it for five hours. Every month the man comes to empty the meter. He takes fifteen bob out of what's in it and gives you back the rest.'

Agnes thought about this. The children waited on her thoughts in silence. Agnes rested her head on her hands and looked down at the table as she deliberated. After what seemed like an hour to the children, she slowly raised her head. You could hear the damp slack as it hissed on the fire.

'All right,' she said simply and the mayhem broke out again. Agnes poured herself another cup of tea and sat back at the table. She stared at the face of her eldest boy. It glowed with joy as he watched Cathy and Trevor dance and sing. Agnes leaned over to him and squeezed his arm. He turned and looked at her questioningly.

'You're a very good boy,' she said with pride.

He got embarrassed and dropped his eyes. 'Thanks, Mammy.'

The telly man installed the telly that night

at seven o'clock. It took some time to fix up the rabbit's ears, but when they were sorted the entire family sat in front of the set, enthralled. There was one problem — if anybody got up to go to the toilet the movement affected the reception. So nobody moved and the ad-breaks now became piss-breaks.

Agnes had a fitful weekend, between the pleasure of the new television and the worry about whether or not she could find the money to get Mark his set of tools. So when she arrived in from work on the following Monday night and Rory handed her the letter that had arrived that day, it might just as well have had the words 'minor miracle' printed on it. It was addressed to 'Mrs Browne'.

She opened it and read:

I. T. G. W. U.
Liberty Hall,
Dublin
Number 4 Branch.
Re: Christmas Benefit.

Dear Mrs Browne,

As the widow of a deceased member of this Branch you become entitled to a death benefit. This is a once-off payment of £12 paid on the Christmas of the year of our member's demise. As your husband worked in the Gresham Hotel, the payment will be available for collection there from the shop steward, Eamonn Doyle, on the morning of the 22nd of December. May I take this opportunity to offer the condolences of the Branch on your loss and wish you and yours a very peaceful Christmas.

Michael Mullen,
Branch Secretary.

'God Bless the Union, and God bless Mickey Mullen!' Agnes exclaimed. 'And thanks, Marion,' she said, smiling and looking up to heaven.

Chapter 22

MARK KNOCKED ON THE DOOR. It was cold, freezing cold. His duffel coat hood was pulled as far up as it would go, and he had a scarf wrapped several times around his neck, but still the cold got through. He knocked again. He heard the movement behind the door, then a click and the door opened a little. Mr Wise's eyes peered out and then the door opened wide.

'Mark! Come in, boy, before you freeze.'

Mark stepped in and Mr Wise closed the door quietly to keep the heat in. They went into the front room where the fire was burning.

'Take off your coat, son.'

'Ah it's okay, Mr Wise, I only called for a minute.'

'Still, take it off or you lose the benefit of it when you go back out.' Mark took it off.

'So, what brings you knocking on my door during the holidays?' Mr Wise sat into his armchair. Mark sat too, but on a hard dining chair.

'Mr Wise — you know loads of people, important people, don't yeh?'

'I do. Some important, some who think they are.'

'Yeh . . . well . . . I want to get me Mammy a ticket for the Cliff Richard concert and I was wondering do you know anyone that could get me one?'

'Who is Cliff Richard?'

'Yeh don't know *Cliff*? Yeh must be the only person in Ireland that doesn't. He's a singer.'

'Oh! Well, I'm not good at names. Now, let me think! Who would I know?' Mr Wise closed his eyes and with thumb and middle finger held his temple. After a few moments he took his hand away and shrugged. 'No! I cannot think of anyone, Mark, I am sorry,' and he looked it.

'That's all right. I just thought you might, that's all.'

Mark started to put his coat on. Mr Wise stood and pointed a finger in the air.

'I have an idea, though.'

'What?'

'Why not get his autograph for your mother?'

'He's auto-graft? What's that?'

'If you go to the theatre, say during the day, with a notepad, he will sign his name on it. I dare say that if you tell him the story, he may even write a little note to your mother too.'

'Would he do that?'

'It's worth a try, isn't it?'

Mark smiled at last. 'Yeh, it is, Mr Wise, thanks a lot.'

Mark buttoned up his coat and Mr Wise went with him to the door. Before he left, Mark took something from his pocket. He handed the colourfully-wrapped parcel to Mr Wise.

'Look, I know you don't believe in it, but here, happy Christmas anyway.'

Mr Wise took the parcel and shook Mark's hand. 'And a very happy Christmas to you, son, thank you.'

Mark stepped out and the door closed. It was just a fifteen-minute walk to the Capitol from Mr Wise's house. Mark walked quickly to keep warm. He was glad he gave the aftershave to Mr Wise — his mother had never used it even once! In Eason's he bought a small notepad, then briskly walked the few steps from there to the Capitol box office. The same girl that had greeted Agnes ten days earlier was there. Mark's head was just visible over the counter.

'Hey, young wan!' he called.

The girl, who had been engrossed in a magazine, looked up. 'What do you want?'

'Tell Mr Richard I want him.'

'What? I will in me shite!'

'Why not?'

'He's not goin' to just drop everythin' and come out to see a little shit like you!'

'Well, all right then, which door is it? I'll go into him.'

'Get yourself away t'be fucked, go on, get lost!'

'Here, all I want is his auto-graft on that.' Mark pushed the little notebook towards her. The girl had gone back to her magazine and she ignored him. Mark persisted.

'Hey! Here, tell him it's for me Mammy,

her name is Agnes. Tell him to write a note.'

The girl leaned forward and called: 'ARTHUR! Arthur, come out here!' The double doors of the stalls area opened, and a huge fat man in a military-style uniform marched out.

'What's up, Gillian?' he asked in a gravelly voice.

'This little fucker . . . he won't go away, he's annoyin' me.'

Mark smiled up at the usher. 'Howye! I need to get Mr Richard to sign this.' Again he held out the notebook. In one swift movement the usher snatched the book, tore it in half, and tossed it into a litter bin in the lobby, and in the time-honoured tradition of the doorman, said: 'Right, son! Fuck off! Go on!'

Mark stared aghast at the litter bin. The usher moved to him and pushed him towards the door. Mark squared up to the man.

The big usher stood legs apart and put his hands on his hips. He saw the anger in Mark's face, and smiled. 'Don't fuckin' annoy me, son, now move!'

Mark's right foot moved quicker than the

usher expected. It made contact, on target, between the big man's legs — Mark could only see his ankle sock as his foot vanished into the man's crotch.

'Ahh . . . yeh little bollix!' the man screamed as his face turned a crimson red. Mark ran to the doors, and into his first problem. Like many theatres, the Capitol had six glass entrance doors, and, like many theatres, only one of these was left unlocked during office hours. Mark could not remember quick enough which one he had come in. He made a choice, the one on the far left. Wrong! The next one — locked! The next one down was the door to freedom, but the usher got there first.

'Right, mister fuckin' hard man, try that again.'

Mark had met his second problem.

By the time Mark reached home his left eye was just about fully closed and had started to change colour from purple to black. The eye had gone with the man's first blow. Mark went down on the cold, tiled surface. The gleaming black leather shoes of the usher had put in the bruises that now covered Mark's back and chest. Mark had limped home. Agnes yelped when she saw the state of him.

'What happened to you?' She ran to him.

'A fight . . . it's nothing.'

'Are you hurt?'

'No, I'm grand, Ma,' he lied.

Dermot jumped from the chair in front of the telly. 'Jaysus, that's a beauty. Who won?'

'It was a draw.'

'Who was it, Marko? Was it Mallet Maguire?' Dermot knew these things.

'No, some fella from Pearse Street.'

Agnes spun towards him. 'You stay away from Pearse Street, they use razors over there, diyeh hear me?'

'Yeh, Ma, I hear yeh.'

Mark went to his bedroom and lay down. Dermot followed him in, and sat on the edge of the bed. He looked at Mark and smiled. 'So, Marko, what really happened? Who gave yeh the hidin'?'

Mark laughed and told Dermot the whole story.

Chapter 23

IT WAS DECEMBER TWENTY-SECOND, and Agnes had lots of jobs for the boys to do. However, Mark and Dermot had an errand of their own to take care of first. They waited in the archway of the GPO. The Garda was standing by the main entrance, where he always stood. The boys waited.

'This'd better not backfire on us, Dermo,' Mark said. He was worried.

'It won't, leave it to me.'

'Make sure you're right beside the copper — right?'

'I will. It'll be all right, just wait and see.' Dermot was confident.

Around the corner, at the same time as yesterday when the two boys followed him, came the big usher from the Capitol, strutting along as if the city belonged to him, a newspaper under his arm.

'Go — *now!*' Mark pushed Dermot. Dermot ran up to the usher and tugged at his coat. The big man stopped and looked down at the boy.

'What do you want?' the man asked gruffly.

'Is this yours, mister?' Dermot held out a sixpenny coin. The man bent to look at what was in the boy's hand. As he did Dermot slapped him as hard as he could with his right fist. The blow caught the giant right in the eye. He instinctively grabbed Dermot. Now it was Mark's turn to kick into action. As planned, he ran for the Garda. Dermot began to scream.

'No! No! Me Mammy told me not to talk to men like you. Let me go . . . I don't want to!'

'You little bastard . . . I'll break your fuckin' neck!' the giant roared, holding on to his now-swelling eye with one hand whilst clutching Dermot firmly in the other. The policeman intervened.

'Unhand that boy!' the Garda said with authority. 'Let him go, now!'

The giant pushed the policeman away. 'Go away, I'll take care of this little fucker me-self.'

The Garda drew his baton, and waved it menacingly. 'Release him right now, boyo!'

The usher dropped the boy. Dermot, in an Oscar-winning performance, hugged the Garda's leg: 'Please, Garda, please don't make me do it. Please keep him away from me!'

'It's all right, son, calm down, nobody's going to hurt you. What's going on here?'

Dermot sniffled and wiped his eyes. A crowd had now gathered around the group and ears were being cocked to catch the whole story.

Dermot began: 'This man asked me to go down the lane with him for a wee-wee!' Dermot cried like a baby. The crowd were not pleased, they began to mutter, and the policeman could envisage an ugly scene on his hands.

'That's a lie!' the usher protested.

'No, it's not, I heard him sayin' it!' Mark came in now. The usher turned towards the voice and saw Mark. 'You? You little bastard!' He lunged at Mark.

Without a moment's hesitation the Garda brought the baton down full strength between the big man's shoulder blades. He dropped like a sack of potatoes. One or two of the crowd poked a bit of boot in here and there. The Garda put a knee into the man's back and handcuffed him with his arms behind his back. In the mayhem, Mark and Dermot slipped away.

The two boys skipped up O'Connell Street, elated with the success of their plan.

'That showed him!' Dermot yelped with delight.

'Yeh! Don't fuck with Mrs Browne's boys!' added Mark, and they both laughed heartily.

They were still abuzz when they came into the flat.

Agnes smiled at them. 'Youse are full of the joys,' she remarked.

'Yeh,' Mark said as he flopped onto the couch. Dermot of course went straight to the telly.

'Yeh needn't think yis are goin' to sit in front of that,' announced Agnes. 'I have work for yis. Turn it off.' Dermot turned the television set off.

'Now, Mark, put Trevor's coat on him and

the three of yis go round to the Gresham and pick up a message for me off Mr Eamonn Doyle.'

'Who's he?' Mark asked.

'He's a steward in the shop, I think. Just ask for him.'

Mark wrapped Trevor up like a bag of rags and the trio set off for the Gresham Hotel. In the streets people were in good festive mood, shouting 'Hello' and 'Happy Christmas' to each other. Christmas is a nice time, Mark thought. Trevor swung like a pendulum between his two brothers, and smiled broadly as he told all who would listen to 'Fuck off.'

The Gresham was a wondrous place. The boys climbed spotless white marble steps and went into the lobby. The massive expanse of royal blue carpet, the gigantic Waterford crystal chandelier, and deep, buttoned leather seating were all things the boys had only ever seen on the movie screen. People were milling through the lobby in fur coats, three piece suits and fancy hats. Mark felt dirty. They stood awkwardly for a moment, and then a woman came out from behind a desk to them.

Mark was expecting a tongue-lashing, but instead she was nice. 'Hello, boys. Can I help you?' she asked with a smile.

'We're looking for Mister Eamonn Doyle,' Mark told her.

'Are you now? Well, it will take a few minutes to get him. You'll have to wait.'

Mark took Trevor's hand again and began to turn him round. 'We'll wait outside — tell him, will yeh?'

'You will not wait outside, it's much too cold,' the woman insisted. 'Come over here.' She brought them to a table around which were four chairs. She called a waiter and told him to get the three boys a soda and biscuits.

Mark panicked. 'Here, Missus — I've no money!'

The woman smiled. 'That's okay, it's Christmas! This is on the house. Just sit there and I'll fetch Mr Doyle. What's the name?'

'Browne, we're all Brownes. I'm Mark.'

'Okay, Mark, you enjoy your soda and I'll be back in a minute.' And she was gone.

The waiter arrived with the drinks and a huge plate of assorted biscuits — pink wafers, chocolate ones with jelly sweets on top, all kinds. Mark gave Trevor one for each hand.

After a few minutes Mr Doyle arrived. 'Hello, boys.'

'How yeh,' Mark answered.

Doyle took a snow-white envelope from his pocket and handed it to Mark. 'There, give that to your mother, and don't hang around here too long.' His disdain was obvious.

'Did you know me Dad?' Dermot asked Doyle.

'No. I don't know many of the kitchen porters.' He was short with them and anxious to be away.

'Well he knew you . . .' Dermot said.

'Good,' the man said and began to walk away.

'He said you were a bollix,' Dermot added.

The man turned. 'What?'

Mark butted in. 'He said thanks a lot, Mister.' The man stared for a moment, and then left without another word.

'Right, c'mon,' Mark said. He stood up and took Trevor's hand.

With his other hand, Trevor was pointing at the elevator.

'Marko . . . bus . . . bus.'

'It's not a bus, Trev, it's a lift, and it's not for us.'

'Let's bring him on it!' Dermot said.

'No. We'll only get into trouble.'

'Ah come on, Marko. One quick trip up and down.'

Mark looked around. Maybe no one would notice. They headed for the lift doors and waited for them to open.

At the same time, Doyle was at the Porter's Desk speaking to the uniformed concierge, telling him about the 'little gurriers', and instructing him to escort them out. The concierge went looking for the boys.

Mark was the first to see him coming. 'Oh fuck! Look, Dermo!'

Dermo followed Mark's gaze and saw the uniformed man looking for them. 'Fuck me, *another* usher!' Dermo was scared now. The lift doors opened. 'Quick, Marko, jump in . . . quick!' Dermo called, pulling Mark's arm.

The concierge saw them just at that moment. 'Hey, you there!' he called out.

Mark jumped into the lift and the doors began to close.

'Which button? Which button?' yelled Dermo.

'Any bleedin' button,' Mark said, and hit the highest one. They saw the concierge's nose disappear between the closing doors. As the lift ascended, they could hear the man banging on the doors below.

'We're in big trouble, Dermo.' Mark was worried.

'I know,' Dermot answered weakly.

The lift stopped on the top floor, and the three boys stepped out into a silent corridor.

'Which way?' Dermot whispered.

'I don't know. Any way except down, I suppose. You go down that end and I'll go this way and see if there's a stairs.' The boys parted, but each made sure the other was in sight at all times. Dermot found the stairs.

'Mark!' he called, pointing, 'stairs!'

Mark lifted Trevor up and began to run toward Dermot. Dermot stepped onto the landing and looked down between the rails.

His heart sank as he saw the peaked cap bobbing as it came up the stairs. It was three floors below. He darted back into the corridor.

'They have it covered!' he cried in desperation.

Just then a door opened on the corridor. A dark man looked out, and in a soft, child-like voice asked, 'Are you all right, boys?'

Mark was silent but Dermot was too scared to be silent.

'The usher's after us, Mister . . . he's goin' to kill us!' he answered.

The dark man stepped into the corridor and took young Trevor in his arms. 'Quickly, get in here!' The boys vanished through the door.

'Excuse me, sir,' a breathless voice called from the top of the stairs.

The man handed Trevor to Mark and put a finger to his mouth. He then stepped back into the corridor. 'Yes?'

The porter was panting. He caught his breath in gulps. 'I'm sorry to disturb you, sir. I'm looking for three urchins, they're on the loose in the hotel. Have you seen them?'

The man thought for a moment. 'I haven't seen any urchins.'

'Thank you, sir,' said the porter and set off on his chase again.

The man closed his door.

'Is he gone?' a muffled voice asked from under the bed.

The man knelt down to speak to Dermot. He smiled. 'Yes, he's gone. The coast is clear.'

Mark studied this man, this hero. He was dark and young, tall, but not fat, and he had kind eyes. Dermot scrambled from under the bed and joined his two brothers in the corner. 'Kind Eyes' spoke. 'What was that all about, or would you prefer not to tell me?'

The boys looked at each other. Dermot spoke first.

'The usher was goin' to kill us because we bashed his mate.'

'No, it's not like that . . .'

Mark interrupted and began to tell his story. Kind Eyes was easy to talk to. The boys relaxed and sat on the bed. Trevor curled up and slept for a while, sucking his thumb. Throughout the conversation, Kind

Eyes would get up and offer the boys a drink or a biscuit or a sweet, all gratefully received. He wanted to know everything, and they told him — about Redser's death, about Marion, Mr Wise, the usher — everything. But mostly about their Mammy.

Before they knew it an hour had passed. Mark jumped when he heard the time.

'Come on, you two, Ma's waitin' for us!'

The boys gathered themselves together and stepped into the corridor.

Kind Eyes spoke softly to them. 'See that door at the end?' The boys nodded. 'Well, that leads to the fire escape. You go down those stairs and nobody will see you leave.'

'Thanks, Mister!' The boys set off. Kind Eyes went back into his room and picked up an envelope from the floor. The address said 'Mrs Agnes Browne, 92, James Larkin Court'. He set off quickly after the boys. At the top of the fire escape he called to them: 'Mark! Trevor!'

The boys were four floors below. They froze.

'What?' Mark called back.

'You dropped this.' Kind Eyes waved the envelope.

Mark handed Trevor over to Dermot and tripped up the stairs. He took the envelope and said, 'Thanks, Mister.'

Kind Eyes smiled and winked.

'Mister?' asked Mark.

'Yes, Mark?'

'What's your name?'

'My name? Harry — Harry Webb.'

'Happy Christmas, Harry Webb.'

'You too, Mark Browne.'

Mark joined the other two and the three sneaked back into the safe, busy streets of Dublin.

Chapter 24

IT WAS A QUIET CHRISTMAS EVE. As it fell on a Sunday, this meant that only a few shops were open, and even those were only open for half the day. Agnes set off early down to Capel Street to collect the tools for Mark. She had the fifteen pounds in her handbag and seven pounds to spare. She strolled down O'Connell Street, taking in the festive atmosphere. At the bottom of Henry Street she stopped for a chat with some of the dealers, out trying to sell off the last of the Christmas wrapping paper. Next she went to the newsagent in Talbot Street, where she bought two hundred cigarettes and a news-paper. She had started buying a newspaper every day now, to see what would be on the telly. She crossed over O'Connell Street again and walked toward Middle Abbey Street. This brought her past the front of the Capitol theatre. As she passed she saw the usher standing in the hallway. He had a black eye and his right arm was in a sling. Poor man, she thought. Then she heard a voice crying: 'Concert tickets! Last of the concert tickets!' It was a ticket tout. Agnes's heart lifted. She went over to him.

'Are they Cliff Richard tickets, love?' she asked.

'Naw, he finished up last night,' the man answered.

Agnes just said 'Oh', and went on her way. So, he had come and gone. Ah well! She got to Lenehan's and paid the balance of her bill. As she made her way home she was filled with the excitement of all the surprises she had for the children.

By six o'clock she had cleaned and stuffed the turkey. The ham was boiling away in the pot, and the trifle was setting in the larder. Two bathfuls of water saw the entire family bathed, as they did it in relays. Instead of calling them to the kitchen, Agnes let the children have their tea by the fire on the floor. The Christmas lights were twinkling on the tree and the laughter of the children at the television programme they were watching lifted her spirits. Agnes began to hum to herself in the kitchen: 'Santa Claus is coming to town . . . Oh you better watch out . . .' There was a knock at the front door.

'I'll get it!' cried Mark.

Agnes wondered who would be calling at tea time on Christmas eve? She went out to see, wiping her hands in the tea towel as she went. Mark opened the door, and for a moment Agnes could not make out who it was.

'Harry!' Mark cried.

Agnes's chin dropped. So did the tea towel.

'Cliff!' she said.

'Hello, Mrs Browne,' he said softly.

'Cliff!' Agnes repeated.

Mark looked from one to the other and shook his head. 'No, Ma! This is Harry . . . he's a friend of ours.'

Agnes was about to topple over and Cliff brushed past Mark to catch her in his arms. Suddenly it all clicked for Mark. He ran to the television and turned it off. Quickly he switched on the radiogram, putting the needle on whatever record was there. It was a Cliff Richard one, of course.

Agnes recovered a little and brushed her hair back. The music played softly. Cliff smiled at her.

'What about a dance?' he asked softly.

She smiled coyly. 'Oh yes!' she said.

He took her in his arms and they began to sail around the room.

The children looked on entranced — Dermot, mouth open, Simon scratching his head in wonderment but knowing something nice was happening, Cathy with her knees tucked under her chin and giggling away to herself, Rory with a tear in his eye, and Frankie standing up slowly as recognition dawned on him.

Agnes looked at her children as she swirled around. The fire glowed on their faces and the Christmas lights sparkled in their eyes. She felt dizzy and a little faint, just for a moment. She closed her eyes and in the distance she could hear Marion give a yelp of laughter, and she laughed happily herself.

Mark slowly and gently lifted Trevor on to his lap.

Trevor laughed and pointed at the dancing couple. 'Harwee?' he gurgled.

'Yeh, Trev, that's . . . Harry,' Mark whispered back.

Trevor smiled and pointed again. 'Mamma?'

Mark smiled a beaming smile and whispered: 'Yeh, Trev, that's her . . . that's our Mammy!'

Sometimes this turbulent, tragic, sad and busy world turns on its head and comes to a sudden halt just to accommodate somebody's dream . . .

Dream on, Agnes Browne! For everyone's sake, dream on!

Center Point Publishing
Brooks Road ● PO Box 1
Thorndike ME 04986-0001 USA

(207) 568-3717

US & Canada:
1 800 929-9108